COMPELLED TO MURDER

E. RAYE TURONEK

DEDICATION

A righteous man falling down before the wicked is a troubled
fountain and a corrupt spring.

- Proverbs 25:26

A MESSAGE FROM THE AUTHOR

This literary novel has been in the works for quite sometime. After originally being writen as a screenplay in 2007, the path for "A Reason to Kill" changed. At the request of a publishing company I began writing the screenplay as a book. Two children later, I finally found the time to buckle down and do what is truly my passion. Much gratitude is given to my wonderful husband for keeping the children busy. Now in 2016, I present to you "Compelled to Murder," the book version of the work previously known to me as "A Reason to Kill." Although I spend my days working as a government employee, I've deemed it necessary to do what I love most. Dedication and drive has allowed me to present you a thrilling literary piece. Bookies, enjoy your read!

- E. RAYE TURONEK

THE BEGINNING

The evening had been nostalgic for them. The moon was full, the stars shone bright. Megan gazed upon the picturesque night sky from the car window as she and her husband John headed home, after a romantic dinner in town. Not a word was spoken as he drove down their street. Words weren't needed, for the love they shared was apparent. In his right hand, he held softly her left. They bestowed upon one another an occasional glance, which exuded the everlasting connection they shared. Once they'd arrived home, John pulled into the driveway. Megan turned to him, glaring into his eyes. A portrait of innocence and vulnerability. Which in actuality, was far from how she felt. Knowing her all too well, he conceded her intense desire.

"So, what's next?"

Radiating a look of assurance, Megan's eyebrow lifted just slightly as she caught the edge of her bottom lip in her teeth. Not being the type of woman to take the role of the aggressor, she preferred subtle sexual advances. Even though, this routine was something he was used to, he is as always, undoubtedly delighted by the thought of her intentions.

John exited the vehicle, walking around the car to the passenger door where Megan waited patiently. As John opened her door, she lifted her right leg from the vehicle, touching her black stiletto to the pavement. Her petite yet long legs were showcased by black sheer silk stockings. Megan reached out her hand. John accepted it, lifting her from the car. The skirt of her short black dress flowed in the breeze as her heels clicked along the paved walkway. "Oh..." Megan lifted her shoulders, rubbing her arms, "I just felt a chill." John removed his suit coat, placing it over her shoulders. "Here you go, my love."

She smiled, "Thank you."

Megan wrapped her arm around her doting husband's, clutching his firm bicep as they strolled up to the front door of their beautiful colonial style home, eager to top off their romantic night. But as they reached the front door their demeanor's shifted in an instant. Realizing door had been left ajar, both glanced at one another with an equal amount of concern. At that moment, the evening had taken a drastic turn. They both took a deep breath as their minds contemplated the worst possible scenarios. Although Megan's heart beat began to thump, John managed to keep calm. He ushered Megan behind him, "Stay back," then proceeded with caution as he pushed the door open wider, remaining a step ahead as they entered. It was dark inside. Sporadic flashes of light from the headlamps of passing cars illuminated the foyer. A quivering Megan stood close to John as he closed the door behind them. "Samantha!" John called out for their daughter.

"Samantha honey, you home?!"

Panic had begun to set in. John's underarms tingled. He was starting to sweat. "God dammit... What the fuck is going on here?!" John yelled in frustration as he flipped the light switch in the foyer. Yet, nothing happened.

"Samantha?!"

Megan tried to stay optimistic, "Maybe she went out."

John walked toward the living room as Megan followed, clutching his arm tightly. He felt along the wall, flipping another light switch. Finally, the living room ceiling fan illuminated. But from the expressions on their faces, it had shed light on the most horrific site they'd ever seen.

Holding her quivering hands over her mouth, Megan belted out an agonizing scream. In an instant, the worry they felt had turned to utter devastation. John's cheeks went pale as the color drained from his face. His stomach jumped into his throat, his body trembled just before his legs buckled, bringing him to his knees. "My God... Sam!!!"

Megan tugged desperately at his sleeve. "Oh my baby.... John help her!"

It was too late, knowing there was nothing he could do to help, John curled over, crying uncontrollably.

Megan wept as their sixteen year old daughter Samantha dangled, lifeless, from a braided noose tied from her neck to the ceiling fan. The fan creaked, wobbling as it spun her naked corpse round in circles. Her eyelids were sewn open, her mouth sewn shut. Barbed wire bound her wrists behind her back. Beyond the black and blue bruising, her torso was severely mutilated, covered with small puncture wounds. It was as if her body had been used as a pinata. A section of skin was sliced from her chest plate in the shape of what looked to be a cross. An overwhelming amount of blood had dripped from her body, forming a blood soaked puddle, staining the beige carpet, leaving her body cold and pale.

Blood spatters canvased everything in the room, the vintage tufted furniture, family portraits, the olive goblet pleated drapes, even the crystal figurines along the fireplace.

Megan went into a fit of rage. She tugged harder at John's arm, "Help her damn it!! Why aren't you helping her?!"

Her words fell on deaf ears. He'd completely blocked her out. Although Samantha was a teenager, to John she was still his beautiful little baby girl, the only little girl he had. She was gone forever. He'd never feel her hugs again, never hear her voice again, and never again get the chance to tell her how much he loved her. John's head hung low, unable to muster the strength to look up. His hands clutched his abdomen as he cried out in horror, "Why?! Why?!"

Tears streamed from Megan's bulging eyes as she dropped to her knees. "MY BABY!"

1

Almost One Year later...

It was just after sunrise when the phone rang, waking John abruptly. Breathing heavily, he lifted his head from the pillow. A generous amount of sweat dripped from his brow onto his prickly ill kept beard. He'd had another bad dream. Like most nights, his dreams were plagued by the heart wrenching lost he'd suffered. John rubbed his hands through his long black hair, sighing not of relief, but sorrow, a sorrow that washed over him like a black flood, carrying him through life, as it was evident that the light in his life had surely burned out. Yet every morning he attempted to bury the emotions his daughter's murder brought about, and go on living life. If you could call it that...

John threw the sheet off of him, then climbed out of bed. Where he now resided paled in comparison to the beautiful colonial style home he once shared with his wife and children. The bedroom in his miniscule one bedroom apartment was in disarray, to say the least. A sea of clothing covered the cold hardwood floors. His dusty dresser was piled with mounds of books and Crimson county newspapers. By the looks of it, one would assume he was researching one of the greatest mysteries known to mankind. Although John's apartment hoarded a mess of clutter, this madness was the calm to his storm. John walked into the living room, disregarding the ringing phone. As far as he was concerned, nothing was of greater importance than what he had planned. He had since dedicated his life to finding the person or persons who savagely murdered his daughter Sam.

The living room was also cluttered with old newspapers. Stacks of books profiling pedophilia, unsolved murders, as well as serial killers, lined the floor along the walls. There was a tack board on the wall with newspaper clippings, detailing the murders of various men, women and children, within a five hundred mile radius of his small town.

John went into the bathroom, then shut the door behind him, leaving the answering machine to pick up the call. John's voice is on the recorder. "Leave a message."

It was Megan, his estranged wife, "John, don't forget, it's your day to pick Shawn up from martial arts. And try not to be late this time." Her voice wreaked of sadness and frustration.

Shawn, the son they share, was the younger of he and Samantha, just a year beneath her in age. Fortunate for Shawn, he was sleeping over at a friend's house the night his sister was murdered. Since the tragic loss of Samantha, Megan thought it best Shawn take up martial arts. That way he'd be capable of defending himself, should a dangerous situation present itself.

Although John loved his son, because he was still reeling over the death of Samantha, he hadn't allowed himself to show Shawn the affection he so desperately needed.

Early that afternoon, John arrived on time to pick up Shawn from jiujitsu. He waited in his old Ford Bronco out front of the martial arts building, entertained by listening to the local A.M. news station on the radio, until Shawn would decide to surface. Pleasant memories of Shawn and Sam's childhood shuffled through his mind like cards. The pair running ramped through the house as little tots, Sam teaching Shawn to swim, Shawn falling off of his bike, Sam picking him up and dusting him off, before she nursed his wounds as a big sister should… Yet again, the memories are tarnished in an instant by memories of Samantha's lifeless corpse dangling from the living room ceiling fan. It was like a candle had been blown out. Just that fast, the pleasant trip down memory lane had come to an abrupt halt, flooding back into prospective the harsh reality of their broken lives.

It wasn't long before he emerged, trotting down the stairs at the entrance of the martial arts building, along with a female classmate who remained just a few steps ahead. Emma was a petite, beautiful, biracial girl with long, curly, sandy blonde hair, which complimented her olive complexion. Shawn happened to be quite fond of Emma. Not only was she beautiful, she was intelligent, as well. And although Emma was a shy, quiet individual, that happened to be a characteristic that Shawn felt set her apart from the other girls in town. Moreover, she was surprisingly capable... something you wouldn't initially gather from her demeanor. Like Shawn, Emma held a black belt in jiujitsu.

Shawn, a very handsome young man, was tall with an athletic build, black wavy hair, and a clean shaven face. One thing about Shawn that intimidated some of the other teens in town was his big, icy, baby blue eyes, which at times made it seem as if he was looking right into your soul. In most cases, a young man as attractive as Shawn would cause the girls to swoon, however, due to his lackluster demeanor toward most individuals it caused the majority of his female peers to steer clear of him. It allowed Shawn to stay low key, which suited him just fine. Emma was one of few exceptions.

"Bye, Shawn." Emma waved as she headed toward her car.

He smiled, glaring at her as she walked down the stairs. "Hey, Emma!" Shawn called out, prompting Emma to do a quick 180 degree turn for him.

"You did great today!"

Emma smiled. "Thanks, you didn't do too shabby yourself! See you soon, okay?"

Shawn nodded in affirmation, and Emma continued on her way to her vehicle.

Since Samantha's murder, she'd been the only person that Shawn had even remotely opened up to. A small part of him was happy when she was around. When they were alone it seemed as if Emma was the only thing that mattered to him. John saw that there was an obvious attraction between the two, nevertheless, they kept their affections for one another private. Emma and Shawn both saw the importance in not making everyone aware of their relationship. Amongst her peers Emma was an extrovert, so not everyone would enjoy seeing her happy, as some viewed her as an easy target for bullying.

As Shawn got closer to his father's SUV, his smile fleeted. A sadness cloaked over him. It was evident that he harbored a great deal of animosity toward his father that he didn't keep secret. Shawn climbed into the truck, slamming the door shut. Before John starts to give Shawn a verbal lashing about slamming the door, he took into consideration the age of the truck, along with the fact that the passenger door wasn't in the best condition. It may have needed to be slammed to completely latch when it was shut, he told himself. John pulled off, neither of them uttering a word.

The tension was so thick you could cut it with a knife. As the awkward silence had begun to bother John, he reached to turn up the volume on the radio, but at the last second he changed his mind, turning the radio off instead. He was well aware that ignoring Shawn would only perpetuate the dysfunction plaguing their father-son relationship. At that point, he decided to initiate a conversation in hopes of Shawn cutting him a little slack. John shook off any residual reminisces of nervousness, then cleared his throat. "So, how was practice?"

But, Shawn was unrelenting. Determined to ignore his father, he pretended as if nothing was even said. John could empathize with why Shawn harbored such a resentment for him, so he was willing to make another go at it. He tried to think of something else to talk about, something that would warrant a response from Shawn. As John glanced down at Shawn's black belt around his waist, he was sure he'd found what would obtain, at the very least, a slight verbal acquiesce. "You must be pretty good."

Even more agitated by the fact that John had waited an entire year before attempting to show any type of interest in his life, Shawn could no longer hold back the urge to acknowledge his father's lackluster efforts. "Ahhh... I get it. Today must be one of those days when you pretend to care."

It wasn't exactly the response he'd hoped for. "You know I care, Shawn."

"Yeah, and bailing on your wife and kid is a stellar way of showing it," he replied spitefully. "Can we just not talk?"

John searched his mind for a viable excuse, however nothing could justify how he'd shut Shawn out of his heart. After all, he didn't cease being a father when Samantha was murdered. Although, his behavior over the past year had reflected that of a man with little obligations. John hadn't spent any quality time with Shawn since Sam had been slain. Shawn didn't even know where his father was living. He'd become somewhat of a stranger to him in just a year's time.

John realized that he may be pushing Shawn to rekindle their father-son bond too fast, without any real effort on his part. A mere talking to definitely wasn't going to do it for Shawn. The reluctance to further pressure his son had slowly kicked in, compelling him to adhere with Shawn's desire to be left alone.

Shawn stared out of the window, tapping his right foot on the floor board in a futile effort to keep his nerves calm. An uncomfortable silence loomed until they reached the big colonial style house, where John no longer resided with his family. By then, Shawn's agitation was at its peak. As soon as John pulled up to the house Shawn hopped out of the truck, again slamming the door behind him, even harder than before. John hadn't even the time to put the car in park, before Shawn was walking up the sidewalk. He struggled for something meaningful to say, but to no avail.

"I'll call you later!"

"Don't bother," he mumbled. Shawn had even neglected turning back to address his father as he responded.

John pulled off mentally exhausted by the encounter. The defeat he felt was something he hadn't allowed himself to feel for quite some time. Even though he hadn't made any headway with Shawn, he remained determined to keep optimistic about his reconnection with his son. After all, he himself had accepted the damage he'd done to their father-son relationship, and was willing to repair it at all costs.

That night under a misty rain, John sat in his car outside of a dive bar, notably waiting for something, or perhaps someone. His desire was to remain inconspicuous that evening. He was cloaked in all black attire in addition to wearing a pair of thin leather gloves. A set of binoculars along with a long lens digital camera laid on the passenger seat beside him.

John sat cursorily examining a stack of pictures of a man leaving that bar, multiple times on different occasions. In the pictures, it was evident that the man was always with a different woman each night. His face was somewhat disfigured. The eyelid on his right overlapped its corner. His smile was crooked due to a very noticeable overbite. Which was why he felt the need to wait, luring in the most inebriated woman at the bar into his clutches near closing time.

It was almost 2:00 a.m. once the man emerged, leaving the bar with his prospect for the night. Like a gentleman, he used his jacket to shield her from the rain. She looked young, in her early twenties. A blonde with a shapely voluptuous figure, similar to the others he'd left with on previous occasions. The girl staggered along, inebriated, as the man helped her to his vehicle, before letting her fall clumsily into the passenger seat. Her dark red lipstick was smeared about her thin lips. Her head slumped into her sloppy bosom. It became all the more evident to John that he was up to no good as he studied the man looking around to search the scene for prying eyes, that could possibly surmise his ill intentions. Still, John went unnoticed. The man hopped into his car, driving off into the night.

John turned his ignition, pulling off, slowly in pursuit. He was careful to remain a safe distance behind, so that he wasn't suspected of tailing them.

Only a few minutes passed, before the inebriated woman was sound asleep. It was then that the man took his chance, pulling into a densely wooded area, following a narrow path that spanned a good distance into the woods. John stopped for a brief moment, turning off his headlights, before proceeding to turn, following them down the path. After about a mile up the road, John observed the man turning off onto a smaller trail. Because his truck was too large to travel the more narrow trail, John decided to stop, and continue on foot.

The man stepped out of his car, again casing the scene to be sure no one else was around, however, the waxing moon provided little light. Surely they were all alone out there, at least he thought so.

By then the woman had come to. Yet still a bit dazed, she looked out of her window. She didn't recognize the area.

"Where are we? Why are we in the woods?"

There was no response to her question, only the sound of crickets chirping. "You said you'd take me ho..." She paused as she'd turned toward the driver's seat, realizing he wasn't there. Instantly rattled by the sight of the car door being left wide open, she lifted her hand, placing it over her heart. "What the hell is going on here?" she whispered. The woman leaned closer to get a better look out of the driver's side door. "Hey!"

"Where the fuck did you go?" She turned to look out of the back window, just as he was closing the trunk of the car. "There you are."

"What's going on here?" she obnoxiously inquired as he hopped back into the driver's seat. She hadn't noticed him slipping the pair of handcuffs into his left jacket pocket. "Sorry about this," he apologized graciously.

The drunken woman was confused, however she fought the urge to overreact, fooled by his disfigurement and kind disposition. "Okay. Why am I not home right now?"

He turned to her, then took a deep breath, licking his lips. His beady eyes grew wide, poised to burst in excitement, "You'll go home after I'm done."

Hastily, he reached outward, groping both her breast at once. His tongue hung from his mouth, primed to savor her teat.

Overwhelmed with disgust, she shoved him away. "Ugh!"

The angry man didn't waste a second, lunging back toward her, only that time with monstrous aggression. He snatched at her shirt, ripping it down the middle. The woman slapped him hard across the cheek. "Hey, you creepy fucker!!"

The slap had not only bruised his face red, but also stunned him to the point of pause. "What the hell is your problem?!" she asked, panting as she clutched her shirt, attempting to hold it closed.

Out of nowhere, he delivered her a hard punch, square in the face. Horrified, she gasped for air, holding her hands up to shield her mouth and nose, while he tore her shirt to shreds. Her eyes beamed wide in disbelief of what was happening. Blood streamed from her nose and mouth, then down her breast plate, painting her torso.

"Okay! Okay! Just stop! Please stop!!" she pleaded helplessly.

But despite her screams of protest, he climbed on top of her. She then realized, she might not make it out of his car alive. The terror jolted an instant wave of adrenaline through her, activating her will to survive. "No! Get off of me!" She pressed her thumbs into each of his eyes. "Ahhh! You STU-PID cunt!" He backed off, covering his eyes with his hands.

That bought her the time she needed to escape from the car, into the drizzling rain. The panicked woman darted off amongst the brush, under the cover of darkness.

His eyes watered, further blurring his vision. Struggling to see, the man rubbed his eyes, blinking until he regained

sight. "AHHHHHHH! FUCK! FUCK! FUCK!" he yelled
in fury as he pounded his fist down on the steering wheel.
She's going to get away, he feared. He hopped out of the
car, ducking off into the brush to hunt her down.

She scuttled through the woods as quickly as she possibly
could, though due to her stilettos catching on loose
branches, moreover sinking into the soft soil, it proved
most difficult to keep her footing. Branches scratched at her
body, leaving rips in her pantyhose and cuts upon her
limbs. Her torso was covered in scrapes and bruises.

She tripped over a downed tree log, taking a nose dive into
a pile of wet leaves. Panicked, she looked left then right,
behind then ahead, trying desperately to see if he'd caught
up with her. There was no sign of her attacker. Still, she
couldn't be sure because the glow from the moon offered
little light. She managed to quiet her breathing, listening for
his footsteps. Again... just crickets chirping.

The battered woman struggled to stand, trying her hardest
not to make a sound. Though in her mind the crunching of
the twigs was magnified, threatening to tip off her attacker
of her whereabouts. She took off her stilettos, then hid them
along the edge of the downed log she'd toppled over, so
that he wouldn't find them.

He tore through the brush, snatching at branches, in search
of her.   "You deserve every bit of what I'm gonna give
you blondie!" he yelled, hoping to draw her out of hiding.

Then, POP! A twig snapped nearby. A feeling of
redemption washed over him. He snarled as he walked up

to the large oak tree just ahead, certain he'd found her. "Gotcha," he blurted, darting his head behind the tree.

To his disappointment, she wasn't there. Again, his frustration mounted. "Urrrrggghhh! Where are you?!"

He turned back, taking a sudden blow to the top of his skull with a steel bat. Blood spewed from the center of his forehead. His eyes rolled back into their lids as he fell to the ground. He took one, two, three, four, five more blows to his cranium. The man was left there, skull smashed in, lying on a pile of bloody foliage. Dead. He never knew what, or for that matter, who hit him.

2

It was around six o'clock in the morning when the sun began its rise. John was seated at the counter, drinking a cup of coffee, perusing the day's paper at the local family diner just down the street from his apartment. Around that time the diner was always moderately busy. The same elderly couples, and single men... usually truck drivers or delivery men, would be there having their breakfast, fueling up at the start of their day.

One of the waitresses, Rose, was a woman in her late fifties. She kept herself busy behind the counter, serving breakfast to the other patrons. Rose had been working at the small town diner since she was a teen. Her dreams of becoming an actress, although quite realized, never came to fruition. Over the years her looks had declined due to decades of abusing nicotine, alcohol, as well as her addiction of choice, prescription drugs. Although Rose was far from the catch of the town, she still liked to think she was the cat's meow.

Behind the counter, the local news was on the television.

John lifted his empty cup, gesturing Rose his way. "Can I get a refill?"

Already ogling at him, she hurried over with a pot of fresh coffee, eager to pour the cup of joe. "Well of course... you know I always take care of you," she said, batting her mascara saturated eyelashes. She poured his cup of coffee, then stood there smacking on her chewing gum. When John finally looked up at her, she grinned, putting her yellow tarnished teeth on display. She'd always thought he was very attractive, but of course, he never noticed her admiration for him.

John turned his attention back to the television. Focused on finding Sam's killer, he hadn't the time to waste on such frivolous things. After all, he hadn't even the time to save his marriage, or for that matter, award his own wife an ounce of his attention. Rose forgave his cold shoulder, figuring she'd try again another day. However, she would stand vigil, serving his needs as the doting waitress.

"Hey Janice, turn that up," she called out to another waitress on duty.

Janice rolled her eyes as she turned up the television, "Yep."

Janice was an attractive woman, only twenty-three, she still had her whole life ahead of her. Free spirited Janice was tired of living out the same old routine. She longed for the day when she would realize her true calling. She had no idea what she wanted out of life. Between babysitting, being a waitress, online school, and writing her blog on spirituality, she found it hard to commit to anything for a substantial amount of time.

There was a breaking news alert on the television that caught the attention of the majority of the patrons. "In breaking news a local hunter has stumbled upon a man's corpse in the woods, just off of River Bluff Trail. The body appeared to have been brutally beaten. Large amounts of the date rape drug GHB had been found in what is assumed to be the victim's vehicle. There are no suspects at this time, however the police are investigating the homicide. The local authorities are unable to release the identity of the victim at this time. We will update you when we have more information. Back to you, Lynn."

Rose then directed her attention back at John. "Lord have mercy. I swear all this madness makes me feel like chum, just floating in the sea, and there's a great white shark out there just waiting to scoop me up."

There was a truck driver seated a few stools from John. He always sat in the same place, but never said much. Every morning he'd have his corned beef with hash omelet, then head out for his daily deliveries. But that day, for some reason, he felt compelled to speak. "Where's Chief Martin Brody when you need him?" he said sarcastically, referring to the movie Jaws.

The trucker's comment hadn't set well with John, but not wanting to ruffle any feathers or cause a ruckus somewhere he frequented so often, he instead took a few dollars out of his pants pocket, then put it on the counter. "Keep the change." He grabbed his newspaper, then headed out the door.

Rose's eyebrows wrinkled. "Well... you didn't drink any of your coffee," she complained despairingly, before lifting his cup to take a look inside. "It was fresh," she mumbled.

Rose rested her other hand on her hip. "What a mysterious fella. Cute too. You know he comes in everyday and doesn't say a word. Just places his order, eats and reads the paper. No matter what, breakfast, lunch or dinner... it's the same thing."

Janice took up his empty plate. "Yes... and everyday you're here gawking at him like a schoolgirl with some ridiculous crush. He barely even notices you're there."

Rose puffed up her chest, lifting her chin. "Oh shut up, girl. What do you know?" Her ego had been bruised before, so she'd live to fight another day. Rose strutted off to the kitchen, sipping the cup of coffee John had neglected to drink.

Later that morning, John walked into his apartment, dropping his keys along with the newspaper on the table in the hallway, before checking the answering machine for messages. "You have one new message."

It was Megan. "John the appointment with the divorce lawyer is tomorrow at 10:00 a.m.. I'd really appreciate you actually showing up." BEEP. "End of messages."

John plopped down on the sofa, considering his options. He'd been a no show for the last three scheduled appointments. If he were missing in action for that one, Megan would surely come looking for answers. Although he'd fallen out of love with Megan, he still cared for her, the thought of what they once shared anyway. John felt that if he officially let go of Megan, he'd be losing a part of Samantha as well. Accepting that was a concept which proved most difficult for him. On the other hand, he knew that he needed to let go of the failed marriage, being that it just created false hope for Shawn. In order for him to come to terms with his parents break up, they actually needed to break up. After sitting there in silence for a couple of hours, John concluded he'd show up to the appointment with the divorce attorney and get it over with. It had already become mentally exhausting. John laid his head back on the couch, falling fast asleep.

Over at the diner, the end of their double shift had finally come. Janice walked through the dining area, turning chairs upside down onto their respective tables.

Rose could be heard back in the kitchen, cleaning dishes. She hadn't said a word to Janice since their interactions that morning regarding John.

"Okay, I've finished up." She removed her apron while she waited for Rose to respond. Yet, Rose didn't acknowledge her. Janice had been riding home with Rose for the past week, since her car had been in the auto shop. I'm not about to beg her for a ride home. Her car wreaks of cigarette smoke anyway, she thought. "I'm leaving then... See you tomorrow!"

Janice took her jacket down from the coat hanger at the end of the counter, replacing it with her apron. "I sure am sorry," she yelled out to Rose as she walked out the door.

Janice strolled off alone into the fog coated darkness, headed home for the night.

"I know you are," Rose whispered as she continued her dish duties. I sure did teach her a lesson, she reveled in thought.

The next day seemed gloomy. A fog from that night still lingered into the morning hours. It was about 9:50 a.m., and John's anxiety was high. He paced the floor in the lobby at the attorney's office. His hands were stuffed in his pants pockets, while his shoulders slumped. It was clearly evident to the secretary that he'd rather be anywhere else but there. "You can go on into conference room one, sir."

John entered the conference room where Megan was already seated at the opposite end of a very long table. "Oh, you're already here."

He took a seat, tapping his knuckles on the noticeably long table. "Nice table," he murmured.

The tension between them seemed to fill the room as Megan remained quiet. Not because she was angry at him. She just enjoyed playing possum, the victim in it all, as she saw it.

Right on time, the sharply dressed attorney entered the room, taking a seat in the middle. Quite fitting, John thought, since he was the neutral party in the situation. This was a case he'd been trying to settle for a long time. Finally he was getting his chance, despite John's efforts to delay it. The lawyer opened their file. "Eh em," he cleared his throat.

"Okay, well this should go relatively smoothly. John, you've already agreed to the terms of alimony. There will be no terms set forth for child support, due to the fact that you'll both equally share custody of Shawn. I assume that's agreeable?

"Yes," John nodded.

"Yes, of course... Shawn needs his father to be there just as much as I am," Megan answered with a tinge of sarcasm.

John's eye had begun to tick, involuntarily. He sniffed, holding his head high while puffing his chest up, in an alpha male fashion. A jab from Megan normally wouldn't bother him that much, though with another man present, it irritated John to his very core. He was well aware of his failures as a father. The attorney being made aware of it, would be down right embarrassing for John.

"Okay then... Mr. Slater wants no part of the house or anything in it, as he's already collected his personal belongings some time ago. So, once the divorce papers are signed by the judge, the divorce should be officially finalized in about forty-five days."

"Eh em," John cleared his throat. "Where is your restroom?"

"Step out of the conference room, and it's straight across the hall on your right, next to the elevators."

"Excuse me." John got up, quickly leaving the room. He tugged at the knot in his tie, loosening its grip on his throat.

The attorney slid the divorce decree across the table to Megan, "Sign on the first X please, Mrs. Slater."

Megan attempted to stall, in hopes that John would re-enter the room, stopping her at the last minute to profess his love for her. She mulled over the divorce decree as if she hadn't already, several times before.

"Is there an issue with the documents, Mrs. Slater?"

Megan looked up, out of the windows that gave view to the hallway. To her disappointment, John was nowhere in site. "No... no... Everything looks in order." Megan signed the divorce papers, then took a deep breath, lowering her head just as her eyes began to tear up.

Just then, the secretary entered the room, "Excuse me sir, the Richards' are here to see you."

Not a moment too soon, he thought to himself. "Excuse me a moment." The lawyer stood, fastening his suit jacket, before he left the room.

John returned just as the attorney was stepping out. He sat down, peering across the table at Megan as if it were her fault that they were even in that current state of irreconcilability. Megan's head remained bowed, considering she'd become noticeably upset.

It was what she wanted. Right? What she'd been pushing for since our split, John thought.

Megan actually thought that if she pushed for the divorce, it would force John into realizing how much he really loved her, convincing him to work at saving their marriage. She thought wrong.

John mustered the courage to speak frankly, "Everything has changed."

Megan raised her head, wiping her tears.

"It's not us who changed, John. It was you. When Sam died, most of you died with her."

The mentioning of Sam from her mouth instantly angered him. "She didn't die. She was murdered. She was brutally murdered in the house you insist on staying in."

Megan's mouth was frozen, poised to respond, except she was at a loss for words. John got up, then shook his head with disappointment before leaving the room. An act he'd carried out for the purpose of causing her shame.

When he'd gotten home, John burst into his apartment, launching the keys across the living room. He paced the floor, mumbling to himself. "I can't believe she had the audacity to even mention Sam. What a low blow."

Soon images of Megan crying, streamed through his brain, pacifying him. He shook his head, regretting his actions. Maybe I was a little hard on her, he thought. "Fuck it," he mumbled, shaking the thought of the entire situation completely.

His mind shifted focus to the manila folder on the coffee table in front of him. He sat staring at it for quite some time before he'd made a very conscious decision to open it, meticulously flipping through its contents. His hesitation was warranted, due to the fact that it was filled with newspaper clippings detailing Samantha's murder. One headline read: LOCAL TEEN BRUTALY SLAIN. There was an image of Sam on the clipping. She looked so much like him, a daddy's girl through and through. Unable to control the rage, atop the devastation he felt, he smacked the folder on the table. His eyes started to water. "COME ON!" The veins in his neck bulged, rushing blood straight to the vessels in his head. His face turned red, while the veins in his forehead pulsated.

"Ahhhh!" John screamed, looking up at the ceiling. "I just need a little help here! Give me something!" he pleaded to God. John sobbed, crying uncontrollably as he rubbed the palms of his hands down his face in a frustrated effort to wipe away his tears. Taking in a breath of air, then releasing it in a long sigh, John gathered his composure. He pondered what to do next. Where did he go from there? I've got to do something, he thought. An idea surfaced, prompting him to rummage through the papers on the coffee table, in search for the local sheriff's number.

At the local police station, the phones were ringing off the hook. Sheriff Laskey, a middle aged African American man in his mid-fifties, was seated behind his desk, busy discussing the issues that plagued their town, with his lead detective.

Detective O'Connell, seated opposite him, was in his late thirties. Although he'd only been a detective for a few years, he was sharp and showed promise.

Sheriff Laskey looked frustrated. He'd been ranting all day, pressing most of his detectives for a lead in the most recent rash of murders.

"We need a break on these murders, O'Connell. People are running ramped in this town, and we're losing control. Without respect for the law and common morality, we can flush our quiet little town right down the commode. People just don't feel safe anymore. Hell, I don't feel safe, and I'm the sheriff."

Detective O'Connell sat up in his chair, "Whoever is killing these women must be changing their method of operation, because now, he, she, or they for that matter, are targeting males as well. That is unless we have more than one killer."

Sheriff Laskey paced the floor, "There has to be, because it just doesn't make any sense, Detective. Think about it. Some of the murders are precise, calculated even. On the other hand, the murders are sloppy and brutally violent, as if the murderer was driven by emotion. There has to be more than one killer. I think our best chance of finding a lead would be with the most violent of the murders. There's bound to be a slip up there. Where there's emotion, there is bound to be confusion."

Detective O'Connell mulled over his suggestion. "Well Sheriff, that could be the case, but we can't rule out the possibility of it being someone who suffers from multiple personalities."

"I'll tell you what... I want more officers on evening patrol. Get word out to every officer that I'm issuing a ten o'clock curfew for all individuals under the age of 18."

Detective O'Connell hopped up from his seat, "Yes sir."

"And be sure to..." The intercom BUZZED interrupting him. It was a female officer, "Sheriff, Mr. Slater's on line one."

The sheriff scoffed, well aware of why John was calling. Although Sheriff Laskey was irritated by the call, it's due partially to the fact that he felt a great deal of guilt for not having made any headway on Samantha's case. John contacting him to check up on the case only compounded the Sheriff's feelings of failure.

"Just great," he mumbled.

"Thanks Officer Sumonher, I'll take it." He sighed, bracing himself before picking up the phone. "Hello Mr. Slater, how can I help you?" he asked, as if he didn't already know.

"Are there any leads at all in Samantha's case? Any developments... even in the slightest?"

"No... I'm sorry, Mr. Slater. We don't have any leads on your daughter's murder yet."

"Come on... Sheriff, it's been a year now. Have you thought about putting a tail on some of the other girls she went to school with, that have similar physical features. I'm really concerned that whoever is responsible for this will attack another girl, and I'm not gonna just stand by while the women in our town are terrorized by some psycho."

In spite of John's argumentative tone, the sheriff listened, biting his tongue until John was finished. After all, it was John's daughter that had been murdered, not his own.

"Look... I know it's hard, but I need you to be patient Mr. Slater. Now, the last thing we need is you going off half cocked and blowing the case. Just let us handle it, and I promise..."

John's impatience had reached its peak, so he'd given into his impulses, disconnecting the call in the middle of Sheriff Laskey's reply.

The sheriff's eyebrows wrinkled. He'd noticed the hushed click of the phone line as John hung up on him. Still, he put the phone receiver to his opposite ear in disbelief. "Hello? Mr. Slater? Mr. Slater?"

"He hung up on me," he acknowledged. The sheriff took the receiver from his ear, checking the button on the phone base that displayed line one. It was no longer lit. He slammed the phone down on its base.

In any other situation, he would feel disrespected by someone hanging up on him so rudely, however, he was sympathetic to John's frustrations, therefore concluding its justification. Sheriff Laskey knew that John's emotions came from a place of deep turmoil.

Detective O'Connell shook his head in disapproval. "Boy oh boy... that guy doesn't give up."

"Cut the guy some slack. I mean... Can you really blame him? Would you give up if someone murdered your kid and strung her up to the ceiling fan in your living room?"

Detective O'Connell shook his head in agreement with the Sheriff Laskey, "You got a point there."

"Of course, I do. Now look, whoever is killing these people doesn't have a criminal record. We can't get a match on any of the fingerprints. Something's gotta shake. I just need these maniacs to slip up one time, so that we can put an end to this. It's starting to tarnish the town's image."

Sheriff Laskey leaned in forward, opening a folder on his desk. "I'm gonna go through these records again. Try to find what it is I've overlooked..."

"It's gonna be a long day," Detective O'Connell proclaimed as he exited Sheriff Laskey's office.

Up front, a woman walked through the doors of the police station. Her eyes scanned the room. She was nervous, on top of being gravely unsure of what she was going to tell the authorities. She looked like a mess. There was a bandage over the bridge of her nose. Her top lip was swollen, along with the bottom being split right down the middle. She braced herself, "Umm, I need to report an attack or umm... a murder... I think," she uttered quietly.

The female officer at the front desk studied her appearance, noticing the small cuts and scrapes on her hands, along with the obvious beating that her face had taken. "Oh my... you poor thing... let me get our lead detective for you."

Exhaling, the woman nodded, feeling somewhat comforted.

The female officer made a call to Detective O'Connell's desk. He saw that the call was coming from the front desk, so he immediately picked up the receiver.

"How can I help you, Officer Sumonher?"

"I have a woman here that needs to see you... Hold on one

second." She covered the receiver with her hand, addressing the woman, "What's your name, sweetie?"

"Jean Becky."

"Jean Becky," the Officer repeated, just to be sure. She found it quite odd, on the count of it sounding like two first names.

"Yes ma'am... Jean Becky," she proclaimed.

She uncovered the receiver, "Ms. Jean Becky needs to file a report... Seems urgent, O'Connell."

"You can send her back to my desk."

Officer Sumonher disconnected the call. "Just head straight back, Ms. Becky. Detective O'Connell will see you now."

Detective O'Connell stood at his desk, waiting to spot Ms. Becky heading his way. She walked clutching her handbag to her stomach as she came into view. He waved his hand high ushering her forward, to assure her that he was indeed the officer she needed to report to.

As Jean Becky came closer, Detective O'Connell had begun to notice her injuries. Although surprised, he remained calm. He'd seen much worse.

Detective O'Connell held out his right hand for a handshake, but only for a few seconds before noticing her hesitation to reciprocate his greeting. Thus, he didn't miss a beat, using the same hand instead, to direct her into the chair opposite his. "Have a seat, ma'am." Some guy has really done a number on her, he thought, as she winced from the aching she felt, attempting to get comfortable in the chair. "So what brings you here today?"

"I saw... ummm... on the news you found a man's body in the woods. I believe it's the same guy that did this to me."

The detective lifted his chin, surprised in regard to what she'd revealed. Yet before he had a chance to reply, she interrupted. "But I didn't kill him. I'm sure of it. I couldn't kill someone."

"Just relax..." Jean Becky took a deep breath, composing herself.

"Now... tell me how all of this happened, ma'am?"

"Well... I can't remember everything. It's all in bits and pieces in my mind, but it's still all a bit fuzzy. Ya know?"

"Are you positive he's the man that attacked you?"

"I mean... I'm pretty sure it's him. I saw his car on the news, and I remember being in that car the night before last. I remember because my friends were supposed to meet me at the bar, but they stood me up... That's why I left the bar with him."

"And, which bar would that be, ma'am?"

"Drifters... The one off of highway M-16."

Detective O'Connell pulled a notepad from his desk drawer. "Okay... I need you to tell me what you can remember step by step. Take your time."

She took a deep breath, then exhaled, before she began to ramble on, recalling the events of that night. "He was hounding me all night. I tried to ignore him, but he just seemed to linger. I don't mean to sound stuck up or anything, but his face was weird... I mean there was something not normal about it. It got late. The bar was nearly empty. I got so hammered... so fast. I don't even remember having that much to drink. He had to help me to his car. I guess I must have dozed off, because the next thing I remember is us fighting in the car. He tried to rape me, but I got away somehow. I ran into the woods. I ran as far as I could. I couldn't run anymore. I started to lose focus, so I leaned against a tree. Then, I... I had to have blacked out because... the next thing I remember is waking up on my porch."

"You can't recall, at all, how you got home?"

Jean Becky nodded, "No... I'm sorry I don't."

"Where do you live?"

"1080 Helper Rd."

"Ma'am... I'm gonna have to fingerprint you."

Jean Becky leaned forward, glaring hopefully into the detective's eyes. "But, I didn't kill him. You believe me, don't you?"

He hesitated, deducing what she'd revealed to him. He indeed believed her story, however, believing her brought about even more mystery as to what was really going on in their small town. Detective O'Connell nodded, "I believe you. But, it's standard procedure in a murder investigation."

Elsewhere, John waited in his truck nearby an elementary school, surveying the scene for something in particular. The kids had yet to exit the building, so John studied the different vehicles that were waiting there to pick up their children. A certain vehicle peaked his attention, one he'd seen before. It was a white van, which sat a couple of blocks from the school. John wondered, if he was there to pick up his child, why would he be parked so far from the school? Especially considering there were ample empty parking spaces much closer to the building.

He'd initially caught John's attention some time ago, when he'd driven by him, on that very same road. Every window on the van was painted over with white spray paint, with the exception of the windshield, driver side and front passenger window. Needless to say, the appearance of the van had peaked John's curiosity enough to follow him. He'd been on John's radar ever since. His intuition told him something wasn't on the up and up so, he waited patiently for the moment his numerous months of stalking would pay off.

The school bell rang, signaling their school day had ended. Children poured out of the elementary school, happy no doubt, to get out into the spring sun.

The man in the white van watched as the children began their trek home. His small beady eyes searched intently, as though looking for his pick of the litter.

He was overweight, but neatly dressed, sporting a white

collared button up and beige khakis. Harmless, right? Or maybe, he just wanted it to look that way.

John watched while the man rode alongside two young boys that were walking up the street, on their way home. He rolled down his window, thus alerting the eldest of the boys of his presence. Right away, the oldest boy nudged the younger, urging him to walk faster.

"Hey, have you kids seen a small gray puppy?"

"No," answered the oldest boy as he stared ahead, being sure not to award him eye contact.

"Well, would you like to help me find him?"

The older boy had a feeling that the man was up to no good. "Don't talk to him," he instructed the younger boy as they picked up speed.

"Dude, you're a stranger. GO AWAY!"

The man floored his brakes, banging on his steering wheel in frustration. Just then, someone else caught his eye, another little boy who happened to be walking alone. This time, he decided to take an alternate approach. He parked his vehicle, then got out intent on not letting that one get away. The man walked down the sidewalk trailing the little boy.

John took out his binoculars to watch, as opposed to following them. He didn't want to get too close too soon, nevertheless he felt the need to keep a close eye on the situation.

"Hey buddy, can you help me?" the man asked.

To his delight, the little boy turned around.

"Who me?"

"Of course you silly, you're the only one around," he responded, while scoping his surroundings to be sure he hadn't garnered unwanted attention.

"Well, what do ya need help with, mister?"

Praying on the boy's benevolence, he bent over about eye level with him, showing him a picture of a small gray puppy. It was obvious he'd done that sort of thing before. Unfortunately, the boy was ignorant as to the man's abysmal intentions.

"I lost my puppy. Can you help me find him? I know he's probably really scared out there all by himself."

The little boy was hesitant, well aware of the dangers of talking to strangers. "I've gotta get home or my mom will be looking for me."

"Come on... It shouldn't take long, if we work together," the man rebutted innocently.

Noticing the boy's lingering hesitation, the man acted fast, sweetening the offer. He pulled out a five dollar bill from his breast pocket. "I'll give you five bucks. Like I said, it won't take long."

The boy's tiny eyes grew wide as he snatched the five dollar bill, staring at it in awe. He was convinced. He'd never had that much money before. "Wow! Five bucks! Okay!" he said, full of enthusiasm.

"My van is back there. We'll drive to look for him... It'll be much faster. Just keep your eyes peeled."

"You sure about this, mister? I'm not supposed to get into the car with strangers."

"Sure, buddy. I'm not a bad guy. Look, would a bad guy give you five bucks? Of course he wouldn't. He'd ask you to help him for free. Now c'mon, we've gotta find Rascal before it gets dark out."

The boy complied, climbing into the van's front passenger seat. However, soon after they'd driven off, the steering wheel began to vibrate. What appeared to be a smoothly paved road felt equivalent to driving along a rocky mountain path. As the man was compelled to pull over, worry instantly kicked in. He clutched the steering wheel tight. Sweat began to roll down his brow. He wiped his hand across his forehead, pondering his next move. I have to get as far away from the school, as quickly as possible, before the kid's parents come looking for him, he thought. He'd already wasted enough time convincing the boy to come along. The man put on a façade, giving the boy a slight grin as he rubbed the back of his neck, edging back further feelings of panic. Still, the little boy could see the anxiety the man was going through, yet he remained ignorant as to why the man was behaving so suspiciously.

"Damn it!"

"What's wrong, mister?" the boy inquired with genuine

concern.

"It's probably just my tire. I think it may be a flat. I'll fix it. It'll just take a second. You just sit here and think about what you're gonna buy with that five bucks."

The man hopped out of the van finding nothing out of the ordinary on his side of the vehicle, but once he'd walked around the front to the passenger side, he found that both tires were completely flat.

"What the hell?!" He thought it odd that both tires would be flat, but he hadn't the time to try to figure out how it could possibly have happened.

He only had one spare, however, the damage to both tires was irrevocable. Trying hard to control his anger, he paced the pavement along side the vehicle. He could no longer avoid pondering how it happened, however he still couldn't fathom a viable excuse.

The little boy was busy admiring his five dollar bill. With his mind transfixed on things he could buy, he couldn't wait any longer. Besides, my mom should be starting to worry by now, he thought. So the boy hopped out of the van, determined to head home.

The baffled man knelt by the back passenger side tire. He noticed that the little boy had exited the van, in spite of that, he remained focused on the task at hand, as there was little time to waste.

"Can you fix it, mister?"

"I'll just be a minute... Get back in the van," he demanded, neglecting to look up at him.

The man's austere tone caused the little boy to become uncomfortable. He slowly began to step backwards. "Hey mister, I've got to get home. I hope you find your dog." Right away the little boy turned, then sprinted off, five bucks in hand.

Flustered, he struggled to stand. "Hey kid, get back here! You little thief!" In a matter of seconds, the little boy was too far gone.

Obesity hindered him from standing quickly from the kneeling position, so of course it wasn't likely he'd give chase. Oh well, I have to figure out how I'm going to fix this mess and get back on the road, he thought.

At the same time, John pulled up behind the van, got out of his truck, then proceeded to approach the maleficent stranger.

"Need some help?"

By then, he was so frustrated, he wouldn't even look up at John. "No, I got it," he uttered in a condescending tone.

"You sure?"

Patience tested, the man struggled to his feet. He stood toe to toe with John. "I said, I got it."

Suddenly John pulled out a .38 caliber revolver, he had tucked in his pants, behind his back, striking the man in his left temporal lobe with the butt of the gun. The man toppled over onto the pavement, much like a tree that had been chopped down by a lumberjack. The blow had caused him to lose consciousness. With a complete lack of frugality, John searched the man's pockets. He pulled a wallet from the back pocket of his khakis, then proceeded to riffle through it, confiscating the man's license in the process. Well aware of his deplorable intentions, John showed no remorse. He returned the wallet to its rightful place, before he got back into the truck, leaving the man laying on the side of the road like a sack of garbage.

That evening at 1016 Cozen Drive, Megan was busy on her laptop, finishing up a work project at the kitchen counter. Her miniature cockapoo, Buttons, laid resting on the counter next to the laptop, watching her every keystroke. She could hear when Shawn came thru the front door, dropping his backpack on the hardwood floor in the foyer. Buttons didn't move a muscle. She was a pampered, lazy pup.

Although Megan was happy he'd finally made it home safe, she was still bothered by the fact that he'd missed dinner. "Shawn is that you? I'm in the kitchen."

"It's me, Mom," he answered as he entered the kitchen, headed straight for the fridge.

"Your plate is in the microwave. Where have you been anyway? We were supposed to have dinner tonight as a family."

Shawn pressed the minute button on the microwave to warm his food, then turned to address his mother. In an attempt at looking bewildered, he widened his eyes, wrinkling his forehead as he nodded, "A family... I just didn't think we'd have enough chairs, Mom."

"Don't be a smart ass, Shawn. In fact, when you finish your plate, I need you to feed Buttons. And be sure to wash her bowl out after she finishes dinner," Megan instructed with a warning note in her voice.

Buttons barked at Shawn, rushing him along. He shot Buttons a stern look, halting her barking in an instant. BEEP BEEP BEEP. The microwave was finished.

"Wash her bowl out? I don't see what the big deal is... You're just gonna put food right back in it. I swear you treat that little mutt like she's a baby," he complained as he removed his plate from the microwave.

"Buttons is most certainly not a mutt. And you know what? I have work to do, so just get it done, Shawn." Megan had concluded that Shawn was in the mood to nitpick, something she most certainly was not mentally prepared for, as a result of her encounter with John earlier that day. So Megan hopped down from her stool, then grabbed up her laptop, quickly making her exit.

Later that evening, John walked into the bar just a few blocks down from his apartment, fully intent on relieving some of the stresses on his mind with a bottle of whiskey. This local bar had been a place for him to momentarily drink his troubles away, ever since Samantha's murder. Happy hour was at seven o'clock, so John usually showed up around ten o'clock or so. In a small town such as

Crimson, most were already home in bed by then. Besides, showing up later minimized the chances of someone ruining his lugubrious mood. Not that anyone could actually brighten his mood, much less have a brief moment to make an attempt at it, without irritating him instantly.

Although it was late, there were still a few patrons lingering about. Dimly lit florescent bulbs in the ceiling illuminated the thin layer of tobacco smoke that remained lingering in the air. A befuddled male patron stood toppled over the jukebox, seemingly perplexed by the many song choices at his fingertips.

The bartender watched him from behind the bar as he cleared empty glasses from the counter. "No more love songs, Jack!"

"Yeah Yeah," he mumbled, before smashing down a button with his index finger, selecting his song choice. HURT by Johnny Cash began to play from the jukebox.

Another man in his early thirties happened to be seated at the bar, two stools over from John. His black thick hair was slicked back. He had a slightly muscular build that was showcased by a tight black v-neck shirt. He was making a real effort to come off attractive, moreover heterosexual, as he guzzled his mug of pale ale. He glanced over at John, deciding to make an attempt at forming a male comradery of sorts.

"Trying to forget something, or is it someone?"

John shot him a quick glance, yet uttered no verbal response.

The bartender was busy behind the bar, towel drying drinking glasses.

"Bartender, can you pour me a double?"

The bartender grabbed a bottle of Jack Daniels, then poured John his double shot.

Excusing John's impertinence, the stranger forged on, attempting to create polite conversation.

"Hey, I'm not judging. We all do or see some fucked up shit. Some of us are doers and some of us are seers. I'm just saying, ya know?"

His comment really rubbed John the wrong way. Even under the influence of alcohol John had a pretty keen sense of awareness. He pondered what the man meant by the, 'some of us are doers and some of us a seers', comment. Had he witnessed me in the act of something compromising, John thought. Unable to shake his suspicions he downed his shot, got up, placed a couple of bucks on the counter, then walked out of the bar.

"By the way, I'm Steven," the stranger mumbled.

Although the antipathy Steven felt toward John was obvious through his eyes, he struggled to tell a different story with his actions. He enjoyed agitating John, nevertheless in the end John got the best of Steven by ignoring him the way he did. He'd actually caused him to feel a tad insignificant.

"Bartender, I'll take a shot of whiskey. A double shot."

Maybe this would help mask the impotence he felt.

After a couple of hours, Steven exited the bar a bit wobbly on his feet. He was mumbling a tune, but you could barely understand what it was he was singing.

John sat in his truck across the street. He'd waited for Steven to surface, in order to get a good look at him, without being too obvious. It was the prime opportunity to do what he did best, so he snapped photos of Steven as he stumbled along to his vehicle.

Steven pulled at the driver's side door handle, but it wouldn't open. Instead his hand slid off, which caused him to stumble backward a few steps. "Whoa," Steven blurted, catching his balance. As he tried lifting the handle once more, he chuckled, amused by how tanked he'd gotten. That time successful, he plopped into the driver's seat of his vintage t-top Camero, then sped off into the night.

3

The next morning, Megan was up making breakfast. She'd woken up early, to ensure she wouldn't miss Shawn heading off to school. The aroma of the crispy, apple smoked bacon frying in the cast iron skillet floated through the house. Fluffy yellow eggs in the plate on the counter were still steaming, just having been poured from the pan. The toast popped up from the toaster, while Megan hummed a tune as she swayed side to side, turning the bacon with a fork. She seemed happy, content at the very least.

Shawn came down the stairs into the kitchen, breathing in the taunting smell of the savory bacon, just as Megan took the last of it from the skillet, placing it on the folded paper towel she had waiting to catch the excess grease. Shawn was surprised his mother was in such a good mood, especially since he'd neglected to clean he and Button's dishes from the previous night.

Shawn took a seat on a stool at the counter, placing his book bag on the empty stool to his right. "Wow... you're in a good mood."

"Well good morning... Of course I am, silly. It's a beautiful day," she proclaimed with a smile.

"Okay," Shawn uttered in a dull whisper. Mornings weren't his favorite time of the day, therefore, he didn't share her delightful mood. His stomach started to grumble, hungry for some breakfast.

"Would you like some breakfast, Shawn?"

"Yes, please."

Megan grabbed Shawn's dinner plate from the night before, scrapping the left over scraps into the garbage disposal. She set it on the counter, putting three pieces of crispy bacon, two pieces of toast, along with a generous helping of eggs onto it. Then Megan placed the plate in front of Shawn.

Shawn's eyes trolled from left to right. He'd felt as if he were in an alternate time zone. What the hell is she doing, he thought. "Ewww... Mom.. you're not gonna wash the plate out?"

"I don't see what the big deal is... I was just putting food right back on it anyway."

Shawn glanced over at Button's unwashed bowl, realizing what lesson his mother was teaching him at that very moment. He nodded his head in affirmation. "That was pretty good, Mom. I get it. Next time I'll wash out Button's bowl."

Although Megan was happy, she was surprised by Shawn's non-argumentative response. She didn't think it would be that easy. "Thank you!"

Shawn looked over at the time displayed on the clock stove. "It's already 7:45. I'm gonna be late. I gotta go," he said, scooping up his backpack with one hand, then the toast and three pieces of bacon with the other.

"Have a nice day," she yelled as he hurried out of the

kitchen.

"See ya!"

Megan made herself a cup of freshly brewed coffee, still steaming from the Keurig. She was home alone quite a bit, since John and Sam were no longer there. With John on her mind, she picked up the phone, calling his place of employment.

"John Slater, please," she asked politely, once the secretary answered the call.

"I'm sorry, Mr. Slater is no longer employed with us. His resignation was accepted months ago."

The news of John's resignation shocked her. He hadn't informed her, that he'd quit his job. At that point, Megan was curious to know more.

"This is Mrs. Slater. How long ago did he resign?"

"Oh... Mrs. Slater, yes... I thought this might be you. He resigned about six months ago. How have you been holding up, by the way?"

A few seconds of silence passed as Megan's mind had begun to wander. How had he been paying his bills, she thought?

"Mrs. Slater, are you still there?" Megan snapped back to reality. "Oh yes... I've been doing just fine, Lori."

"I'm sorry, Mrs. Slater... I have another call. I have to answer it. You take care now," the secretary said, with a tinge of disappointment in her voice. Since having gotten wind of their divorce being in the works, Lori had been waiting to find out her share of gossip as well.

When Megan hung up the phone, her mind overflowed with unanswered questions. Why would he quit his job? What has he been doing all this time? Why wouldn't he tell me? John's work situation had provided her, yet another reason to see him. After all, she wasn't over him. Nor had the pain of her marriage ending subsided.

Later, around 3 p.m. the school day had just come to a close. The bell sounded at Long Lake High School, releasing the students from their classrooms. Shawn exited the front doors of the building, almost immediately spotting John sitting in his truck, waiting for him no doubt. "Here we go again," he whispered as he walked over, climbing into the passenger seat. Shawn had a wall up over his feelings so high, he acted as if the damage done to their father-son relationship was irreparable.

But, John was determined to put forth his best effort, to mend the relationship he had with his son. Normally he wasn't picked up from school, so of course, Shawn was curious as to why John was there.

"Stuck with me again, huh?"

John brushed off the sarcastic comment. That day he wasn't going to allow Shawn to start an argument. "I figured I'd pick you up today. I wanted us to spend some time together."

Shawn glanced at him from the corner of his eye. He'd

never admit that he longed for his father's attention, as any child would. Yet still, even in spite of the current situation, he didn't want to come off too eager. He'd been let down too many times, by John in particular.

"So what's the plan?"

A slight grin came upon John's face as he shifted the truck into drive, "You'll see."

The pair remained silent throughout the twenty minute drive through their small town. They passed by the main post office, where everything was business as usual. Neighbors stood chatting on the sidewalk, just before going inside to mail off their packages. There was a play ground next to the post office bustling with children, kicking around a soccer ball, as others took turns pushing one another on the swings. The scenery started to change as they came closer to their destination. Soon the road converted into a two lane highway, followed by dense woods becoming evermore present. The road's edge was lined with trees that had just recently sprouted their lush green leaves. Shawn knew exactly where his father was headed. He used to take he and Sam there quite often, before it all went sour.

Shady Point Pier was a late night hangout spot, popular with the local teens. Though it was indeed a place where they could swim while partaking in alcoholic beverages, along with other illegal substances, it also served as a fishing spot by day.

John pulled up along the beach, parking right next to the

pier. "You remember this place?"

"Of course I do. You used to say it was our special place."

"It still is, Shawn," he proclaimed as they both exited the truck, grabbing their fishing poles and tackle box from the hatch back. Ready for an afternoon of fishing, they walked along the pier to find a good spot.

"Let's go all the way out to the end. That's where the good fishing is," John suggested, eagerly walking ahead.

Once John and Shawn got their lines into the lake, the tension between them seemed to fade completely.

"Ya know, last time we did this the fish caught you."

"Yeah, well back then I was still a snot nose kid. Besides, maybe today is the day I get my revenge."

All of a sudden, John felt something tugging at his line. "I think I got one!"

He started to reel it in, when his line got snagged on something down below, "My line is caught." John tugged even harder on the rod, but still unable to free his line, he gave up. Besides, he didn't want to break his fishing rod. "Ahhh, it's no use... Shawn, do me a favor... hand me my knife out of the tackle box, will ya?"

Shawn riffled through the tackle box, pulling out a curved, sharp, stainless steel blade. Impressed by his father's choice in cutlery, his eyes widened.

"Whoa! Now this is a pretty impressive blade, Dad."

"You want it?"

He raised an eyebrow, shocked that John would let him have something so potentially dangerous, then thought, he's got to be kidding. Shawn chuckled a bit, "Are you serious? Mom would choke on her pumpkin spice latte." If it were a mystery before, it was definitely clear then that his father was trying way too hard to get on his good side.

John looked left then right, in a joking fashion. "I don't see her, I guess the coast is clear."

Shawn hesitated, waiting for his dad to change his mind.

"Seriously... go ahead, take it. I trust you to be responsible with it. Grab the holster for it as well though... I don't want you stabbing yourself while trying to shove it into your pocket."

Shawn quickly grabbed the holster from the tackle box, then slid the knife inside.

"Hey, Shawn?"

"Yeah, Dad..."

"You mind if I use your knife to cut this line?"

They both chuckled as Shawn realized he'd put the knife away prematurely, "Oh yeah, sorry. Sure you can... no problem."

"I've also got an extra tackle box for you," John informed him as he cut his fishing line free. The look of admiration on his face granted John a feeling of comfort he hadn't felt in a long time. Our father-son time is coming along wonderfully, he thought.

After a little more fishing, the two headed home. Once they'd pulled up to the big house on Cozen Drive, Shawn hopped out of the truck, satisfied with how his day had turned out. To John's amazement, he'd even refrained from slamming the passenger door. "See ya."

"See ya later, son." It had been a long time since he could utter those words comfortably.

As Shawn was walking toward the house he did a quick spin, calling out to John before he could pull off. "Hey, Dad... Thanks!"

"Thank you... son," John replied, holding back tears of joy. He drove off, releasing a huge sigh of relief. He'd been stressing about how the unplanned visit with Shawn would turn out. In that very moment, John found it unbelievable how much valuable time he'd missed with his son. He began to busy his mind thinking of other things they could do together. Hunting, sailing, even camping, had all become a possibility, since they were getting along so well.

Late that night, an unidentified person carried an unconscious Janey Harris, a local teen, over their shoulder, down a long dark corridor in the basement of an old abandoned warehouse. Water leaked from the pipes in the ceiling onto the cement floor. Her arms dangled effortlessly, much like her long, wet, stringy, dirty blonde dyed hair.

They entered a dimly lit room. One of the two long

florescent light blubs buzzed as it flickered on and off. Janey's body was flung down onto a cold cement slab. In the process, the back of her head knocked against a low hanging light fixture.

The stranger grabbed a standing AMSCO operating room light from the corner of the room, positioning it carefully over her body. As she laid unconscious, her wrist and ankles were bound in restraints. The stranger removed her blindfold, while she remained passed out cold. Wanting her to be completely aware of what was going to happen to her, he grabbed a bucket of water that had collected from one of the leaking pipes in the ceiling, then splashed it into her face. Janey awakened disoriented, frantically coughing and gasping for air, at which point she realized she'd been tied down. Fear immediately coupled with confusion as she looked around the room, struggling to pull her arms free.

"What the fuck?! Where am I?!"

The assailant was considerably larger than her, yet had a masked face, so she had no idea who it could be. He was dressed in navy blue auto mechanic coveralls with black boots. He covered his dirty hands with blue latex gloves, waiting patiently for the moment Janey would break out into absolute panic.

"Who are you? What the hell is going on? Let me go!!! Help!!! Somebody, help me!!!"

It was only a matter of seconds, until her fright had indeed become sheer panic. Veins bulged from her neck, turning her face blood red as she screamed, struggling to free herself. The assailant knew no one could hear Janey screaming, a fact that only brought him further gratification. He started to move closer, but as his face neared hers, she laid flat, clutching both sides of the cement slab with her hands. Janey wept helplessly, turning her face away from his as he slowly licked her cheek, taking his tongue up the side of her face to taste her tears. He rubbed his erect penis back and forth along her hand. "Noooo!" she hollered out, disgusted by the perversion of it all. "Stop it!!!"

The assailant chuckled, as he was quite amused by her furry. "I digress," he uttered in a deeply mumbled tone.

Instead, he grabbed the duct tape, prompting her to plead for her life. "Please don't do this! Just let me go! I won't say anything!" He taunted her with a strip of tape, moving it closer to her mouth, then farther away again. "Please... Please... I promise," she vowed mercilessly. Finally, he duct taped her mouth, muffling her pleas for mercy.

A tray of immaculately shiny surgical tools, which included a pair of scissors, a bone saw, toothed forceps, a skull chisel, a bread knife, a scalpel, rib cutters, an enter-o-tome, and a stryker saw, were on a table along side the cement slab.

Whomever it was, they weren't planning to go easy on her. She trembled as the harsh reality of her death being imminent started to become clear, unveiling a look of sheer horror in her teary bloodshot eyes.

The assailant grabbed a pair of scissors, cutting Janey's

shirt open. She wasn't wearing a bra. "Mmmm," he moaned, aroused by the sight of her bare breast. He paused, rubbing the nipple of one of her petite A cup breast with the palm of his hand, then began mushing it round and round. Her eyes bulged, watching the assailants every move. She breathed heavily, still struggling to free herself. But, to no avail. He cut her daisy duke jean shorts straight down the middle, revealing her white lace bikini underwear. Then he grabbed a scalpel, slowly cutting the outline of a cross out of the skin on her chest plate. By then her screams had become so violent, she'd managed to loosen the tape from her mouth.

Enjoying every minute of her torture, he proceeded to carefully peel back the skin as she yelled in agony.

Still, he wasn't satisfied. So he slipped on a thicker pair of cotton gloves over the latex, before drifting off into the darkness for a few seconds to grab a roll of barbed wire from the corner of the room.

Janey shook her head, almost losing consciousness. Although she dreaded what was to come, at the same time, she was afraid that if she allowed herself to black out, she'd never wake up again. The assailant began at her bare feet, slowly wrapping the barbed wire tightly around her body as she screamed in pain.

She could struggle no longer, for it only caused the barbs to dig deeper into her flesh. The loss of blood had weakened her. "Please... Please," she whispered. It was a futile attempt at begging for her life, however it was the best she could do at that point. Janey's blood leaked from her open wounds, trickling down the cement slab, painting the floor red.

4

The following day had come. It was exactly one year ago that Samantha Slater had been brutally slain. Her father John walked through the cemetery, carrying a bouquet of yellow tulips. Eighteen tulips to be exact. Which was the age she would've turned that year, had she still been alive. Once John made it to the plot where she was buried, he placed the bouquet upon her tombstone. Sunglasses covered his tearful eyes. Yet, they could not mask the devastation he felt as the tears began to stream down his face, soaking into his ill kept beard. John's head hung low as he sat on the ground with his back resting against the side of Samantha's tombstone.

The headstone read: OUR ANGEL ON EARTH CONTINUE TO BE AN ANGEL IN HEAVEN, SAMANTHA SLATER, GONE BUT NEVER FORGOTTEN

Although she was gone from them in a physical form, he felt her spirit still lingered there with her remains. Speaking to her was something he had to do, in order to maintain some sort of sanity, amidst the madness that had become his life.

"Everything has fallen apart, Sam. We're just not a family anymore without you. I was afraid to admit it, but you and your brother were the only things that kept your mom and I together. I tried so hard to hide it from you guys. Still, I think you knew. My baby girl, you knew me better than anyone."

John tilted his head back, resting it against the tombstone. He sat there silent, for a moment, wishing that life hadn't turned out the way it did. Wishing he could turn back time...

"I'm gonna find out who did this to you, Sam. I'll never stop searching until I do. I promise you that, baby girl. They'll get what they deserve."

By around 4 p.m. that afternoon, John was at the local diner having some lunch, while he took in the local scenery from the window next to his booth. He scarfed down the last bite of his club sandwich, when out of nowhere... BANG BANG BANG, a vagrant pounded the side of his fist hard against the window. Some of the other patrons jolted from the loud noise, then turned their noses up at the dirty beggar, once they'd realized where the raucous had come from. John, however, wasn't the least bit startled. He shot the vagrant a blank, eye piercing stare.

The vagrant had become accustomed to receiving nasty looks, so John's stare down hadn't bothered him in the slightest. In fact, he decided to yell his request right through the glass. "Hey mister, got some change?!"

Still, John didn't say a word. When the silent treatment finally got to him, he flipped John the middle finger, "Well fuck you too, asshole!" Sprinklings of saliva shot out of his mouth, then onto the glass.

To his surprise John didn't even blink. The vagrant scoffed, curling his upper lip as his eyebrows wrinkled. "Psycho!" Finally, he walked away empty handed.

Well look who it is, John thought to himself as he noticed Steven exiting his Camero across the street. Steven headed straight into the town's only hunting supply store. The male clerk sitting on a stool behind the counter was aware that Steven had entered the store and casually began to browse, but he continued quietly reading his hunting magazine as Steven approached the counter. There were a plethora of weapons on display along the wall behind the counter, various types of bows and arrows, rifles, swords, hunting knives, even shot guns. Finally, the clerk put the magazine aside, rising from the stool to do his duty. In the clerk's opinion, Steven didn't look like the hunting type. There was just something he found metro-sexual about him. Maybe it was the gelled hair or the form fitting v-neck t-shirt. He wondered what Steven could possibly be there to purchase.

"See anything that interests you?"

"I see you've got some pretty high tech crossbows. Any of them any good?"

The clerk nodded. "Yes indeed... I think we can find something fitting for you." The clerk took a crossbow down from the wall, placing it down on the glass counter top. "How about this one, The Penetrator. It's reliable... You don't even have to adjust the scope."

Steven picked up the crossbow and began to look it over, pulling at the drawstring, then testing the trigger.

"That one's a real beauty. Just pull that trigger and your target is a done deal," the salesman said, figuring Steven was an amateur at best.

He aimed the crossbow, pointing it toward the diner, as if he knew John was there watching. "Nah... this isn't quite what I'm looking for." After a few seconds, Steven lowered the crossbow, placing it back on the counter. "That's what I'm looking for," he affirmed, pointing at another crossbow hanging on the wall. "What's the draw weight on that one?"

The clerk turned to look up at the crossbow Steven was referring to, but before he could answer Steven's question, Steven continued. "I'm guessing it's about 270. That's more my speed. I can adjust the scope myself. I see it has a four arrow quiver. That's real nice. How light is it?"

The salesman raised an eyebrow, surprised by his knowledge. "This is the Nightmare 335, it's for experienced hunters... which I'm guessing you must be, since you seem to know quite a bit," he admitted, taking crossbow down off of the wall, before handing over to Steven.

Again, Steven aimed the crossbow toward the diner, this time looking directly at John, through the scope. He watched John, picking at his teeth with a toothpick as he studied Steven's Camero from the diner window. "Yeah... this is the one I want."

"So, what's your sport? What do you hunt?"

Steven lowered the crossbow, giving the clerk a serious look. A look solemn enough to cause the clerk to become a tad weary of him.

"I've got a bitch I'm trying to get rid of."

"A bitch?" Shocked by Steven's reply, the clerk threw his

head back, raising his chin.

Steven set the crossbow down on the counter.

"This time of year they run crazy, rummaging for food in my yard. I can't have coyotes roaming my property."

"Oh..." The clerk belted out a sigh of relief that faded into slight chuckle. "A bitch. I get it. Well, how do you know it's a female?"

"She has her pups with her, and you know... nothing beats the taste of a young one."

Again, the clerk was confused about the look on Steven's face. Yet even then, he still shook his head in affirmation, going along with his every word. At that point, the clerk was just trying to get him out of there.

Steven shook his head, laughing at the absurdity of his comment, "I was being facetious. I don't really eat coyote. Do you?"

The clerk wasn't really sure whether he believed him or not, but he was definitely ready to be out of Steven's company, so he hastily began to ring up his merchandise. "So, will this be all?"

"For now."

Across the street, already seated in his truck, John commenced spying on Steven as he exited the hunting supply store with a large box in hand.

Steven tossed his box through an opening in the roof of the

t-top Camero, onto the passenger seat, before he got in and drove off.

John followed him, keeping a good distance behind until they came upon an abandon apartment building at the edge of town, where Steven stopped, eventually ducking off into the building. John was sure that something wasn't right about the whole situation. Why would Steven be going into an abandoned building that's been empty for over a decade, he questioned. John snapped pictures of the building along with its grounds before pulling off.

Early the next morning, John lounged on the couch in his living room, drinking a beer while he gawked at the television. His insomnia had been plaguing him more often than usual, as of late. Maybe it was his brain creating a defense mechanism to keep him from having to deal with the horrible dreams he would suffer. Then again, it could have been the anniversary of Sam's death that was keeping him from sleeping. John flipped through the channels, finding nothing of interest, until he came upon the local news. He stopped, in hopes of seeing something that would bring him purpose. Not that he wanted to see innocent people hurt, he just craved feeling of use.

A male news anchor reported directly from the scene, "Tragically, the body of an eighteen year old girl was found in the woods behind this abandoned saw mill. The body has been identified as Janey Harris, a senior at Longfellow High School, who was reported missing last night. If anyone has any information as to who could have committed this horrible crime, please contact the local sheriff's office."

"Son of a bitch!" John launched the television remote across the room.

Just then, Shawn crossed his mind. Not considering the time, he picked up the phone, calling to check on him.

Over at the big house, Megan opened her bathroom door, walking lethargically back to her room, before climbing into bed. Just as her eyes closed, the phone rang, startling her. She closed one eye while squinting the other, in order to see the time displayed on the clock atop her nightstand. It was almost two o'clock in the morning. "Ugh... you've got to be kidding me?" Megan turned on her bedside lamp, then reached for the phone.

At first, she fumbled with the receiver, attempting to get a good grip on the phone. It was loud, and she didn't want the noise to wake Shawn. Agitated, she finally answered.

"Hello," she whispered.

"Megan, where's Shawn?"

"John? It's two o'clock in the morning. He's home sleeping, of course."

"Well, can I talk to him? It'll just take a second."

"Are you serious?"

"Please Megan..."

She let out a deep sigh. "Hold on. Give me a second."

Megan threw back the blanket, climbed out of bed, then headed down the hall toward Shawn's room, cordless phone in hand. Once she reached his bedroom, she knocked at the door, "Shawn."

There was no response, however, being that Shawn had been known to ignore her a time or two, she doesn't find it unusual that he hadn't responded. Megan didn't want to start an argument, which was sure to happen if she opened his door without his acknowledgment, so she called out a bit louder. "Shawn, your dad is on the phone!" Still receiving no response, she was prompted to open the door. To her surprise, his bed was empty. "He's not here," she whispered, baffled, by her findings. Megan put the receiver back to her ear.

"Oh my God... John, he's not here," she blurted in a more realized tone.

"Damn it..." Although John shared Megan's concern, he rathered not put her in a panic. "Don't worry about it. I'll find him. He's probably just hanging out with some friends."

"Friends at this hour?!"

"Go back to sleep, Megan," John instructed, before quickly hanging up the phone. The last thing he wanted to do was waste time going back and forth with her.

A few blocks over from Megan's residence, some of the local teens had congregated at a fellow classmate's house. It was the usual teen house party, which of course meant, no adult supervision. Several empty beer cans laid scattered across the front lawn. Inside, teens were chatting amongst one another, drinking beers, smoking marijuana, and listening to music... Music so loud, that the teens had to yell just to hear one another.

Two girls stood in the corner immersed in meaningless conversation. One of the two was Shannon, a popular, redheaded cheerleader, the head cheerleader in fact. She happened to be the girl most of the guys in school tried their hardest to impress.

The other was Jennifer, a brunette, equally popular, rich and attractive as well, but she wouldn't be caught dead with a high school boy, a fact that was well known amongst her peers. Their maturity level was not of her standards, so most of the guys saw her as a prude, an unobtainable prude. And of course, all the boys wanted what they couldn't have. Jennifer personified herself as if she were God's gift to mankind, and gossip happened to be her favorite pastime.

"Did you hear about Janey?"

Shannon sipped her beer from her plastic red cup. She could care less about Janey, or anyone else for that matter. "No. What about her?"

Just then, another teen stumbled up, awfully inebriated, nevertheless he was still drinking. Eric had all the characteristics of a dumb jock, cute, muscular, overly moussed hair, self-absorbed, and pushy as well, which irritated Jennifer in particular. He lurked there, listening to their conversation. Jennifer rolled her eyes, somehow managing to refrain from making a rude comment toward him. After all, it was a party, and he had just as much of a right to be there as she did. The more he leaned in closer toward her, the more she leaned toward Shannon.

"The police found her dead body in the woods behind the old saw mill. Her body had been mutilated."

Eric finally chimed in. "She was such a hillbilly. Her boyfriend probably chopped her up, so he could eat her."

Simultaneously, Shannon and Jennifer's heads' turned toward Eric, looking at him as if he were a fly that had just landed on their food.

"She wasn't chopped up, you idiot. She had puncture wounds all over her body. And if her boyfriend was gonna eat her, they wouldn't have found her entire body lying in the woods," Jennifer replied.

"Hey, that's just my opinion."

"And you do have a right to your opinion, but I also have the right to tell you how stupid your opinion really is."

"Dude, chill out. How do you know what happened to her anyway, Sherlock?"

"It's been on the news all day, you dick. Oh I forgot, you don't use your brain cells to retain useful information."

A sardonic smile reached across to the corners of Eric's mouth as he grabbed his crotch, brushing against Jennifer, "Yeah, I got a big one just for you."

She scoffed, pushing him away. Nothing could be more

revolting to her. "Ewww! Back off, you horn dog."

"You know you want it."

"I wouldn't sleep with you if you were the last man on earth."

"Yeah right, give me the zip code to the state of denial. I'll send you a postcard."

Jennifer wasn't amused by his sarcastic comment. "Whatever, I don't have time for this. I need a drink," she said, walking off to the kitchen.

Shannon was a little tipsy at that point, so she just stood there with a smirk on her face. Now Shannon was in no way, shape or form attracted to Eric, it was just a tad amusing to her that he irritated Jennifer to that degree. Although she and Jennifer were best friends, Shannon was well aware that Jennifer thought she was better than everyone in high school, just because she didn't date high school guys.

Shawn was planted on the sofa in the living room smoking marijuana with his best friend Dillon. Dillon was a major league pothead, in fact, he was the host of the party.

Shawn coughed, squinting his blood shot eyes after he puffed the joint, "Man, this is actually some pretty good shit."

"I know, dude. I lifted it from my step-dad." Dillon grinned proudly, nodding his head, but not really changing the permanently dopey look of his face.

Shawn passed Dillon the joint as he stared over at Jennifer and Shannon. The two were again huddled in the corner, too good to mingle with the commoners.

"Dude, do you even know half these people?"

Dillon blew a huge puff of smoke, then passed the joint back. "Nope, but if you say party they will come," he announced with his arms sprawled out, as if he were welcoming all to come.

Shawn exhaled and the two chuckled, simultaneously. "Alright dude, fun time is over. I gotta get home, before the warden notices I'm gone."

"Dude, your mom keeps a leash on your ass."

"I know, right?" Shawn agreed as they bumped fists, before he got up to head out the door.

Another hour went by, before the party had finally begun to clear out. Jennifer was just getting ready to call it a night, but had been intercepted by another guy at the party. Her decision to entertain his conversation was influenced purely by her need to give her buzz time to wear down. The guy was a real geek, the school mascot, in fact. His physical attributes were short and scrawny. You'd think his confidence would be diminished for those reasons alone, however, that was clearly not the case. In an attempt at getting fresh with her, he rubbed his hands across the gold crucifix pendant on her necklace as he gazed into her eyes. "I've had a crush on you since the 7th grade, you know?"

It was at that point Jennifer decided she'd rather take her chances getting home tipsy. Besides, it's not like I'd be driving drunk, she thought. Backing away, she distanced herself at arms length, "I'd better go."

Nevertheless, he remained optimistic. "Do you need me to walk you home?"

Feeling as though she couldn't get out of there fast enough, she hastened her efforts to escape his advances, slowly walking backward.

"No. I live pretty close. I can just take the path through the woods. I'll be there in no time. Thanks, anyway..."

Jennifer turned forward, continuing her exit through the kitchen. The teens had made a mess of things. There were plastic cups, used plates, empty beer bottles and pizza boxes scattered over the granite counter tops and island in the center of the kitchen. She turned up her nose at the clutter as she headed out the back door. That was a close one, she thought. It was still dark out, so she hurried through the backyard, hopping the chain link fence.

Although taking the short cut through the woods was a normal practice for her, as it was for most of the teens in Shady Pointe, that time was much different. Unbeknownst to her she had company. Someone watched as Jennifer walked casually through the woods. POP! A twig snapped startling her. She stopped dead in her tracks, looking around to see if anyone was there. The night sky coupled with all of the hallucinogens she'd consumed, made it appear to her as if the moon were eclipsed.

"Is somebody there? Hello?"

No one responded, nor did she hear anything else, so she continued on her way. Then, an owl hoots, making the journey through the woods she'd taken so many times before seem foreign, and more eerie than it had ever been. "I knew I shouldn't have smoked that shit," she mumbled.

POP! Again, a twig snapped, that time spooking her to the point of chills. She looked back, then all around her doing a complete three hundred and sixty degree turn, Jennifer was sure someone had to be there.

"Who the hell is that?!" She could hear someone's footsteps shuffling through the dead foliage, but figured it was one of the immature high school boys from the party, just trying to spook her. Maybe it was the school mascot repaying her for thwarting his advances. "Ya know what, grow up!!"

The footsteps sounded even closer with every step, yet she was finding it difficult to tell what direction they were coming from. With what happened to Janey crossing her mind, she became panicked. She took off, running full speed ahead with her arms stretched out in front of her, pushing through low branches and shrubs as she glanced back ever so often, to ensure she wasn't being chased. At last, she'd reached the road's edge. Jennifer stopped. Panting as she bent over, resting her hands on her knees, she allowed relief to wash over her. The sight of her house just across the road brought her comfort. "Idiots..."

"Ugghhh," she exhaled, exhausted by the entire ordeal. I can't wait to get to bed, she thought.

Jennifer stood up straight, when suddenly, she was snatched back into the trees by her hair. The assailant dragged her effortlessly through the woods as she gripped the assailant's gloved hands. Kicking and screaming, she tried to free her hair from the attacker's clutches.

"Let me go!!! Somebody help me!!! Help!!!

Jennifer was loud, and having grown tired of her pleas for help, the assailant flung her through the air, as if her weight were equivalent to that of a small child. Her body slammed against a large oak tree, knocking the breath from her lungs. Jennifer's limp body crashed to the ground. Even then, she managed a feeble attempt at getting away from her attacker, struggling to crawl as the assailant loomed over her. Fighting the pain and fear she felt, Jennifer managed to steady herself on her hands and knees, but a swift kick in the butt sent her back to her belly. With no fight left in her, she laid there crying, face down in the leaves.

"Please... Please... Why are you doing this?" she asked desperately. It was the last thing she uttered, before being bludgeoned in the back of her head with a boulder. Blood oozed from her skull as her attacker nudged at her hip with their foot, forcing her over onto her back, solely for the privilege of watching the life drift from her eyes. Finally the assailant dropped the boulder, before kneeling only to snatch off her necklace, taking it as a trophy of sorts.

E. RAYE TURONEK

5

Late the next morning, Shawn came down the stairs headed for the kitchen. Smoking all of that marijuana had caused him to be more than a little hungry. When he entered, Megan was standing at the counter pouring herself a cup of coffee. She was relieved that he'd made it home safely, yet disappointed that he'd even pull such a stunt, after all she'd already been through. Shawn opened the refrigerator and began weighing his options. There was bacon, eggs, sausage, frozen waffles, strudel, and many other options to choose from, all of which required more effort than he was willing to exert at the time, so he grabbed an apple instead. Shawn chomped into the big, juicy, red apple, as if he hadn't eaten in years. "Someone's dropping the ball," he commented sarcastically, still having no idea that she knew about him being out til the wee hours of the morning. Megan starred into the murky depths of her coffee, whirling her teaspoon about as she waited for him to close the refrigerator door, which would be her cue to start in on him.

"Where were you?"

The question caught Shawn off guard, so he stood there frozen, unsure of exactly what his response should be.

Megan moved toward him, trying to keep her calm, "I looked in your room at about two o'clock in the morning. Needless to say, you weren't there."

Shawn dropped his arms down to his side, belting out a

sigh of agitation. He was sure to droop his shoulders, just so Megan got the full affect of his exasperated sentiment. "Here we go again," he mumbled.

He'd grown tired of her fake, overly concerned act, and it was written all over his face. He'd come to realize that she'd never see how embarrassed he was of her affair. Or maybe she just didn't care, a possibility that really boiled Shawn's blood.

"I was over at Dillon's house. He had a few people over, and I told him I'd stop by. No big deal, Mom."

His arrogance, coupled with the flippant nature in his stature, immediately angered her. "No big deal! You know you're not allowed to be out that late. Let alone without permission." Megan sighed, shaking her head as she held tight to what little empathy she had left. "Shawn, I don't understand why you insist on breaking the rules," she said, having lowered her voice.

"Come on, Mom. Take a chill pill. I'm not Samantha. Nothing's gonna happen to me. Besides, Sam was at home when she was murdered. You do remember that fact?"

Megan was disgusted by his blatant disrespect. Her eyes had begun to tear up in disbelief. She found it difficult to fathom him having the gall to utter such hurtful words. Megan flung her right hand back over her shoulder, before launching it forward, slapping him hard across the left side of his face. The cup of coffee dropped from her left hand to the floor, shattering the mug and spilling the coffee across the porcelain tile. The sting of her strike traveled from his cheek up to his eyeball, and although the entire side of his face burned red, he managed to hide how much it really hurt.

"Way to go, Mom. There's nothing like some good old fashion child abuse to bring us closer together," he grumbled furiously with a chided expression, before storming out of the kitchen.

Megan stood there speechless, but visibly shaken. She began to lose her balance, but caught herself by leaning against the stainless steel refrigerator. Her jaw dropped, in awe of what had transpired. With one hand she clutched the handle tight, while using the other to cover her gaping mouth.

That afternoon, John cruised down a residential street, before slowing to park across from a sitting mail truck. He took out the license he confiscated from the man's wallet, matching the address to a small blue house on the block. Then, John drove two houses down the street, so he had a clear view of the man's home, but at the same time could avoid alerting any suspicions. He didn't have to wait there long before the man surfaced, exiting the front door of the small blue house. He watched from his rear view mirror as the man headed to his white van parked in the driveway, rubbernecking left and right for anything out of the ordinary. John slumped down in the driver's seat, ducking from sight. The man hopped into his vehicle, driving off right past the truck, still unaware of John's lurking presence.

Once the van had driven by, he sat up, slowly peeking his

head over the steering wheel. The white van was just bending a right at the corner of the block. The coast was clear. John exited his vehicle, headed straight for the backyard. Toys were scattered across the grass. John concluded that if no children actually lived there, it was evident that certain measures had been taken in an effort to ensure children felt comfortable around the home. Once John reached the back door, he peeked inside through a small window. It was quiet, and all the lights were out, so he put on a pair of black leather gloves before attempting to enter. John turned the knob. It was locked. Of course that was to be expected. Prepared for a B&E, he took a small pouch of tools from his jacket pocket. In all of thirty seconds of using his tools, John had gotten the door unlocked and was stepping inside the house.

First, he moved through the immaculately clean kitchen. There were no granite counter tops, nor any stainless steel appliances. The cabinets and tile were outdated, to say the least, but it was spotless. He continued through to the living room, which was spotless as well. So far, there were no signs of a child living in the home. Fishing for something to validate his suspicions, John headed up the stairs, just off of the hallway. There were three doors to choose from, all of which happened to be closed. With caution, John opened the first door on his right. There was always the possibility that there could be someone else in the house. But if there was, they weren't in that bedroom. Something wasn't quite right though. It looked eerily similar to a motel room. There were no family portraits or photos on display, no personal artifacts of any kind, just a neatly made bed, a nightstand and dresser. John opened the closet, but it was empty, so he decided to dig a little deeper. He walked over to the nightstand and opened the drawer. It was at that moment his heart sank into his stomach, as he'd seen the drawer was scattered with photos of young children. John lowered his head in disgust. The children were scantly dressed, none posing for the camera, but all looking either frightened or embarrassed. He shuffled through the pictures almost losing his stomach, once he realized that most of the children in the photos were students of the nearby elementary school. John was livid. He slammed the drawer shut. How could someone do such a thing, he thought. Proof positive, he'd found what he came for, John stood ready for what came next.

Just then, the man came through the front door, brown paper bag in hand. Oblivious of John's presence in his home, he went into the living room, then plopped down on the recliner, directly in front of an old floor model television. He grabbed the remote off of the end table next to him, and changed the channel to a baseball game. Next, he grabbed a beer from the brown paper bag, opened it and took a few big gulps. The man felt pretty relaxed as the excess beer leaked from the corners of his mouth down his double chin, dribbling onto his gray t-shirt. With his eyes glued to the television, he dug back into the paper bag pulling out a bag of plain potato chips. "What the..." he murmured, squinting his eyes, attempting to recognize the reflection he saw in the television. He couldn't see what it was right away, yet his eyes grew wider as they adjusted themselves, revealing what the reflection happened to be. Alarmed, he quickly tried to stand, nevertheless it was too late. John had already wrapped a thin metal wire around his pudgy neck. He strangled the man, while he struggled to snatch the wire from gripping his throat. The chips were knocked to the floor during the struggle. The beer spilled over, running down the table, soaking into the brown shag carpet. The man gawked at his reflection in the television as he witnessed his life being strangled from his body. When John removed the wire from his throat, his tongue was left hanging from his mouth and his eyes wide with shock.

John's job there was done. He pulled out the license from his pocket, tossing it onto the coffee table, before he made his exit. One less predator roaming the streets while he searched for his daughter's killer, was how John justified it.

6

Meanwhile, Shawn was laying on a couch, going through his weekend therapy session. Linda Schwartz, a soft spoken psychiatrist in her mid-forties, was seated in the chair across from him. At that juncture in their sessions, Linda had come to the conclusion that Shawn had some deep rooted issues due to his family situation, as well as the tragic death of his sister. However, Shawn had a knack for stonewalling, furthermore, he possessed no desire to be fixed.

"I'm worried about you, Shawn. It's been a year since your sister was murdered, and you haven't shown any progress. I really need you to open up. Trust me. Tell me how you feel, Shawn."

Shawn had absolutely no intentions of granting her request. After all, why would he? In his experience, trusting people hadn't resulted in the most favorable outcomes.

"Why did your husband leave you, Linda?"

Even though, the hurtful question was a low blow to her ego, she was used to that kind of insubordination, so Linda remained focused, brushing off Shawn's rude inquiry.

"It's Mrs. Schwartz, Shawn, and we're here to talk about you, not my personal life. Why don't you tell me why you're so uncomfortable talking to your female peers?"

Linda struck a nerve, purposely of course.

"You expect me to open up to you, and I can't even call

you by your first name. Why don't you call me Mr. Slater then, Mrs. Schwartz?"

"Shawn, I can't release you until you've shown a sufficient amount of progress. Now come on, be straight with me."

Lucky for her, the slap he'd endured that day had encouraged him to reveal his true feelings. Shawn sat up on the sofa, looking her directly in the eyes, his elbows rested on his legs with his fingers intertwined.

"Straight. Here's straight. My mom is an overbearing, self-righteous slut. Who by the way, has been cheating on my dad since I was fifteen, but of course she'll deny that to her grave. My non-existent father finally got wise and ditched her when the only child he really cared about was slaughtered. And my sister, well let's just say you shouldn't speak ill of the dead."

Although Linda was shocked by his admissions, she doesn't let on. It was definite progress, however, his response wasn't quite what she expected to hear. She'd decided that she would need some time to regroup, before responding to Shawn's briefly subtle rant, plus she didn't want to push him too far.

"Okay... I think that's enough for today."

He quickly stood, confidence regained, as he was relieved that she wasn't intent on moving forward with the conversation. "I thought so... See you next week," he said as he headed out of Linda's office.

It was about 6 p.m. that evening, when Megan came

through the doors of a casual dining steakhouse. The lighting was dim and a melody from a soft jazz piano could be heard playing over the sound system, which made the ambiance of the restaurant something to be admired. She walked clutching her black handbag with one hand and tugging at the hem of her short periwinkle dress with the other, as she had begun to worry whether or not its length was appropriate for that venue. Her black strappy heels caught the eye of the hostess as she approached the counter for information regarding the whereabouts of her already seated party. "Oh, I love your shoes... And that dress... What a beautiful color," she remarked.

"Well, thank you," Megan flipped her long hair with poise.

"You're quite welcome. Now, how can I help you?" Before Megan could answer, the hostess interrupted, "Welcome to La Pointe, by the way."

"Yes... Thank you... I'm supposed to be meeting someone here, Ron Sturgess is the name."

Ron was John's best friend, or at least he used to be. The fading of their friendship coincided with the downfall of John and Megan's marriage.

"Oh yes, right this way. He's already here waiting for you." The hostess lead Megan to the table where Ron was seated. As Megan and the hostess approached, he stood to pull out the chair for Megan. He was a short handsome guy with a chiseled physique. His curly blonde hair and piercing gray eyes were hard to resist.

"Have you been waiting long?"

"Not at all," he replied, gesturing his hand at the chair for her to take a seat.

Once she was close enough, Ron leaned in for a kiss, but Megan turned her face, causing the kiss that was meant for her lips to land on her cheek instead. Feeling the sting of her subtle rejection, Ron pushed her chair up close to the table, leaving her little room to move about once she'd taken her seat.

"Eh Em," the hostess cleared her throat, having taken notice of the awkward moment. "Your waitress will be over shortly," she said, before leaving them in each other's company.

Ron took his seat across the table from Megan, "I ordered you a glass of Pinot Grigio."

He came off sweet, as well as charming, however, looks can be deceiving. He was actually a conniving pervert, who preyed on the insecurities of naive women. Characteristics such as loyalty, chivalry, and honesty were not something he practiced. Megan knew this all too well. After all, she shared the same defects in her character, yet she remained reluctant to acknowledge that fact.

"Thanks. So why are we meeting here?"

"Well, I figured we needed to talk. I've been calling your office. You're never available. I'm starting to feel like you're avoiding me," he huffed, as if even the thought of that being the case was an impossibility.

"No. I just have a lot on my plate right now with Shawn

and the divorce."

Ron saw a glimmer of hope in her excuse. "So, he signed the papers?"

"Well... no, not exactly," she grudgingly replied.

Ron reached across the table for her hands in an effort to provide her emotional comfort, yet even then she pulled back. Once again put off by her slight undertones of rejection, he angered instantly.

"What's going on with you, Megan? How can you sit here and act as if we haven't been sleeping together for the past two years? I'm the one who was there for you when Samantha died. Hell, even before that. Not him... Do you even want a divorce?"

"Of course, I do. I'm just worried about him." At that point, Megan didn't even know if she believed what she was saying.

"You're worried about him," Ron shook his head with disappointment. "I'm not going to play second fiddle to John anymore. Either you get the divorce, or I'm gone."

Because she'd really bruised his ego, Ron wanted to put on the pressure, so he got up, threw his cloth napkin down on the table, then stormed off before she could even respond. Megan saw that the female diner of a couple seated at a table in the immediate vicinity had taken notice to the slight temper tantrum, pointing it out to her male companion. The embarrassment she felt in that moment caused her to hesitate, allowing Ron to make it halfway out of the restaurant's entrance, before she was prompted to react. "Ron!" She called out to him, but was too late. He continued on his way out the door.

Well after her work day was done, Linda decided to spend the latter part of her day at a local tavern. The very same one John frequented, only hours earlier than he'd normally show up. She sipped a cocktail in hopes of relieving some stress. A vodka straight up with an olive should definitely do the trick, she thought.

Steven was there as well, seated one stool over from hers, chugging back a mug of pale ale. "You here to drink your troubles away, too?"

She smiled, "Oh no, I just came to relax."

"That's some heavy relaxation. It most certainly should do the trick." He extended his hand to her, "By the way, I'm Steven."

She reached her hand over the empty stool, reciprocating his greeting, "Nice to meet you, Steven. I'm Linda, Linda Schwartz."

"So, what's on your mind, Linda Schwartz. If you don't mind me asking?"

"You can call me Linda."

"Okay. So what's on your mind, Linda."

Of course, being a psychiatrist, she believed in expressing her feelings as opposed to bottling them inside. Therefore, Steven's question had bestowed upon her the prime opportunity to do just that.

Linda sighed, thinking, she was going to need another drink for that conversation, but maybe she should tone it down a little. "Bartender, can I get a glass of chardonnay?"

The bartender was standing close by, already listening in on their conversation, of course. "Coming right up, beautiful."

"Well, thank you," she replied with a smile, before turning her attention back to Steven.

"Steven do you have any children?"

"Nope, but I used to be one," he answered, jokingly.

Linda chuckled. "Yes, of course you were. Let's see... how can I explain this, while staying within the boundaries of doctor patient confidentiality? Okay... Well anyway, let's just say I know someone who has been through a lot within the past few years. Consequently, it's caused him to hate himself, as well as his family. I don't know if I should speak to his parents about it. He may see it as an act of betrayal. Not to mention, I'd be compromising his rights to confidentiality. On the other hand, if I don't speak to them, I'm afraid he could become suicidal."

"So, you're a doctor?"

The bartender placed the glass of wine in front of her. "Of sorts. I'm a psychiatrist."

"Well, you have to ask yourself, is the boy's life worth saving."

Linda was a bit disturbed by his comment. "What kind of question is that to ask yourself?"

Steven found amusement in the fact that he had caused Linda to be uncomfortable, and he'd been made well aware by the contrite look upon her face.

"It's an honest one," he rebuffed, while giving her a stone cold, eye piercing stare.

Fearing she may have gone too far by divulging so much information about her unnamed patient, Linda collected her belongings preparing to exit. "I really shouldn't be talking to you about this. It was nice meeting you, but I'd better go. I've got a long day ahead of me tomorrow." She placed the money for her drinks on the bar, "Enjoy the rest of your night, Steven."

Linda rushed out of the bar, headed straight for her car. It was exceptionally dark out due to the fact that some of the street lights weren't working. Good thing she was parked right out front, so she hadn't far to walk. Linda got into the car, tossing her purse on the passenger seat. She waited there for a moment, brooding over Steven's bizarre comment, before she started her car, then began her journey home. Unable to shake the thought, she continued steering with her left hand, but reached over to her purse with her right, fumbling through it in search of her cellular phone. She was so preoccupied with finding her phone, that she didn't even realize her car careening across the yellow lines in the center of the road. She was about to cross paths with another vehicle on the opposite side of the road. But just as the driver in the oncoming vehicle laid in on their horn, it startled her, bringing her attention back to the road just in time to avoid collision. "Ahhh!" Linda swerved back to her side of the road, having successfully retrieved her phone, and although her heart was still pounding, she breathed a sigh of relief. "Oh my gosh..." Being the analytical person she was, Linda had begun to think of all the things that could have happened because of her careless driving. I could have killed someone... I could have killed myself, she thought. She shook the negative thoughts from her mind, continuing on her way home, only this time waiting until she pulled into her driveway to fiddle with her phone. Once she shifted the vehicle into park, she dialed Shawn's mother. It rang a few times before going to voice mail, so she left a message. "Hi Mrs. Slater, this is Mrs. Schwartz. We really need to discuss some things regarding your son, Shawn. Please give me a call as soon as you get this. My number is 555-2800."

At last, she'd made it home safe. Linda grabbed her purse, then exited her vehicle. Stepping out too quickly, she rolled her ankle, almost completely losing her footing, but managed to catch her balance by hanging onto the car door. She paused for a brief moment, in an effort to regroup. Linda hadn't realized the drinks had taken such a toll on her.

"Okay," Linda took a deep breath, composing herself, before she continued to her front door. Soon, she has another misstep on the stairs as she was headed up the porch. "Urggh," she huffed, quickly brushing it off. Linda was so relieved once she'd made it inside, she leaned against the door, dropping her keys and purse onto the floor in the foyer. She removed her pea coat, letting it fall onto the floor beside her. Finally, she kicked off her high heel shoes, which took flight across the foyer. These were all things she wouldn't normally have done before her separation, however since Linda lived alone, she could do whatever she pleased. After a long day's work, she would normally head straight up the stairs to the bathroom for a shower, therefore not wanting to get too out of character, Linda does just that. She turned on the water in the shower, testing the temperature with her hand. It was just right, so she undressed, then stepped into the shower. Trying to sober up a bit, she leaned her head back, allowing the water run down her face, soaking through her short, brown, bobbed hair.

Once she'd washed the smell of cigarettes and alcohol from her body, her shower was complete. "Ahhh," she moaned feeling refreshed. Linda grabbed her plush, pink bathrobe, hanging on the back of the bathroom door, then wrapped it around her water drenched body. She wiped the steam from the mirror on the medicine cabinet, staring with a look of non-complacence. Years of stress and abuse, combined with aging, had brought about the appearance of crows feet along the edges of her eyes. She'd always felt ugly throughout her adolescence, however, since she'd been separated from her husband her insecurities had resurfaced, affecting her even more so than ever before. Linda opened the medicine cabinet, taking out a tube of wrinkle reducing cream, and like she'd done every night, she applied a generous amount around her eyes. "I'm definitely not getting any younger," she complained, examining her reflection closely. Out of nowhere, a spontaneous yawn caused her to realize just how exhausted she really was. "Oh goodness, I'd better get to bed," she said as headed to her bedroom, just a couple of doors down the hall.

Linda opened the bedroom closet, and out of nowhere, her cat jumped out from the top shelf. "MEOWWW!"

"Ahhh," she screamed, raising her hand over top of her chest as she watched the cat scurry off. "Minkzy!!! You scared me."

When she turned back to the closet something slowly dawned on her. How did the cat get trapped in the closet in the first place? Someone had to have shut Minkzy inside the closet. Maybe her ex-husband had been there, she guessed. He hated cats, especially Minkzy. She was always in the way. "How did you get in the closet?"

Suddenly, a masked assailant, cloaked in black, lunged at her from behind the hanging clothes. "Oh my god!" She screamed in terror as the assailant plunged a butcher knife into her shoulder blade. Although the pain felt disabling, pure adrenaline allowed her to react instantly. She grabbed the assailant's wrists and they began to struggle. But, the assailant was much stronger than Linda. She was forced backwards, eventually falling onto the bed, with her attacker over top of her. She used one of her hands to lunge for the phone on the nightstand, but because she was waving so frantically, she knocked it onto the floor instead. The attacker wrapped his left hand around her throat, while the knife was pierced deeper into her shoulder. Her face flushed over red as the air was cut off from her lungs. Fighting for her life, Linda crashed her knee into the assailant's groin. This bought her some time. Released from the attackers gasp, she coughed, gasping for air as she stumbled out of the room, clutching her shoulder in an effort to slow the bleeding.

Linda trudged to the top of the stairs, tripping over the cat. She tumbled down the stairs, slamming onto the hardwood floor in the foyer. "Oh God," she groaned from the pain of the fall, before looking toward the top of the stairs in a panic. No one is there. She touched her hand to her forehead, "Ouch." It was bleeding. Linda feared she hadn't much time left to make an escape. She turned to the front door, but something was different. Her coat was still there on the floor, yet her keys and purse were no longer there where she'd dropped them. Linda struggled to stand. Once she was finally to her feet, she limped to the living room in search for something she could use to defend herself with.

The house was dark, but the street light in front of her house provided her just enough light to guide her through the room. One of the living room windows was up, allowing the nights gentle breeze passage through the opening, which lifted the ivory sheer curtains through the air. Linda grabbed an antique cavalry saber sword, her ex-husband left mounted on the wall above the fireplace. She turned back, quickly holding it up as her defense against attack. Still, no attacker. Linda limped over to the dining room table, but grabbed the cordless phone off of a side table, on her way there. Now I need some place to hide and fast, she thought. She lifted the white linen table cloth, crawling under the dining room table. She started to dial 911, but just then, she heard footsteps prompting her to pause. She could hear the sound of the front door open, then close. Although her heart felt as if it were pounding through her chest, she waited silently, until all was quiet, before she proceeded to dial 911. She put her ear to the receiver. There was no dial tone. "No, no, no... shit," she whispered.

Linda placed the phone down with ease. Just then, she remembered something. She'd put her cell phone in her coat pocket. Linda carefully lifted the tablecloth, but only enough for an eye to peek out, looking around to be sure the coast was clear before coming out from her hiding place. No one appeared to be there. She clutched the sword as she crawled from under the table, then moved cautiously to the foyer. With one hand she grabbed her cell phone from her coat pocket, still clutching the sword tight with the other.

Out of nowhere, the cat ran between her legs. Startled, she dropped the phone, then wheeled the sword down, slicing the cat in two. Oops. Her jaw dropped, horrified by what she'd done. Minkzy had startled her last human. Within seconds, her expression went from extreme regret to relief of the fact that she wasn't being attacked by the intruder. "Damn it, Minkzy... you kinda had that coming," she mumbled. Linda knelt to pick up the cell phone, realizing it was broken. Could things get any worse, she wondered. "Why is this happening to me?"

At that point she felt that there was no other option, but to get out of there. Preparing to open the front door, she took a deep breath, then held the sword up high, ready to slice whatever got in her way. Although she was reluctant, it was what she had to do, so she slowly turned the knob, then quickly jerked the door open.

You know how it is when you go to the hospital, and they use that translucent tape to hold your I.V. In place? It hurts so much to take it off that you have to brace yourself, then just rip it off really quick. Then, the hair on your arm comes off right along with it. Yeah... that's how it was. Linda just needed to get it over with. Anyway, back to the story...

No one was there. Feeling somewhat relieved, she lowered her sword. It was at that moment that the assailant caught her off guard, leaping from the side of the porch. Repeatedly, he plunged the knife deep into her chest, taking her breath away. She was in such shock, that her eyes seemed to bulge from their sockets. Linda managed to belt out one agonizing scream before death took hold. She fell back onto the foyer floor, face to face with Minkzy.

7

That next morning as John walked down the hall of his apartment building, he saw Megan waiting by his door, manila envelope in hand. What does she want now, he asked himself.

Megan held up the envelope, "You left the lawyer's office before you could sign the divorce papers," she blurted, before he had an opportunity to question her motives for being there.

Although her mere presence agitated him, John wanted her out of his apartment as quickly as possible, for more reasons than that alone. He accepted the folder from her, unlocked his door, then headed into the apartment. Megan followed close behind him, afraid that if she didn't, he'd close the door in her face, leaving her standing in the hallway. John didn't want her roaming through his apartment, so he put his keys on the side table near the front door, then grabbed a pen from the drawer. The last thing he needed was for her to find out what he'd been up to, and go off blabbing to the authorities. Megan peered over him as he leaned over to sign the documents, but glanced up occasionally, noticing the disarray he called a living room. There were more than a few empty beer bottles scattered about. The remote was broken on the floor in the corner of the room. Newspapers and books were spread across the coffee table in front of the sofa. John maintained an emotionless silence as he signed the papers, then handed them back over to Megan. She was sure he'd show some form of resistance, but clearly, she thought wrong. Her feelings were crushed. "That's it. You're not gonna say anything?"

John was reluctant to travel down that road with her for more valid reasons than were needed, so he said the first thing that came to mind, in an effort at thwarting off her advances. "How's Shawn doing?"

"Shawn is being Shawn, as usual," Megan replied. At last she'd gotten him to start a conversation, at which point she quickly took her chance, changing the subject.

"I called your job, they said you quit months ago. What have you been doing all this time?"

John shook his head in disbelief of the fact that Megan insisted on prying into his personal affairs. "And how is that any of your business?"

She hesitated as she looked around at the clutter in his apartment, slowly coming to the realization that she had no right questioning him, for she was one of the reasons it had come to this. Her voice softened, "I'm worried about you, John."

He wasn't buying the concerned wife act, nor was he swayed by the apologetic expression upon her face. "So worried that you had to rush those divorce papers right over, huh?"

The fact that she wasn't getting through to him had begun to frustrate her. "What do you expect? What do you want me to do, John? Wait around forever?"

John scoffed, not only appalled, but fed up with her spoiled, self-righteous demeanor. "I expected you to be a loyal wife. Not screw my best friend like a whore, but I guess that was too much to ask a person of your moral fiber."

You could say, those in her circle had always filed her indiscretions in the unspeakable category. Besides, John himself had already gone so long, never actually verbally acknowledging her affair with his ex best friend, that Megan surely wasn't expecting him to respond with such harsh words. She hung her head in shame, unable to muster the gall to look him in the eyes. "You know, you don't have to insult me like that, John. I am still the mother of your children."

"You're right. I shouldn't have insulted you by insinuating money was involved. Whores get paid. You were a volunteer prostitute."

His comment twisted like a knife in her gut. Megan looked up at him, eyes beaming in disbelief. "Look John... there's no need to regale yourself with my failures as a wife. Don't you think I've beat myself up enough about this? Besides, I didn't come here to argue. I... "

John interrupted before she could continue what he thought was sure to be a self-pitying response. "You're right... You actually got what you came here for, and now I think it's time for you to leave."

A lump formed in her throat as she fought back tears of regret, however, with nothing to say that could possibly furnish a valid excuse, she stormed out of the apartment embarrassed, defeated, and even worse, unwanted.

Elsewhere, Dillon ventured out getting a late start to his day. He exited the back door of his house, rocking out to tunes from his iPod. As usual, he hopped the fence, then walked casually through the woods behind his house. Dillon played the air guitar, thrashing his head about, leaving him ignorant as to his immediate surroundings. All of a sudden, he stumbled over something that sent him crashing to the ground. The earphones fell out of his ears. "Fuck dude..." Dillon lifted to his knees to dust the leaves from his clothing, but paused, realizing his palms were covered in blood. "What the fuck?"

He glanced back, seeing something which terrified him to his very core. It was the dead body of a female, laying there amongst the brush. "Ahhh!!! Holy shit! What the fuck?! Holy shit!" Panicked, he quickly crawled several feet away from the corpse, before actually rising to his feet. "Okay... Okay... Okay... Okay," he chanted, in an effort to somewhat calm himself. "Ugh," he shivered.

Yet, even though Dillon was repulsed, he was curious as to the identity of the lifeless woman. So he gathered the nerve, then slowly walked back over to the corpse. Due to the fact that some time had passed since her death, loose foliage had already covered the majority of the body. She was lifeless... her fingers were broken and twisted, still shielding the back of her skull. Dillon bent over, then began brushing the leaves from her face. However, because the blood had saturated her hair, clumps of dried leaves were matted onto her scalp. He had no alternative option, other than to peel them back from her skin. His hands trembled. He lifted his shirt over his nose to mask the overwhelming stench of rotting meat. Almost losing his stomach during the process, Dillon remembered something. He hadn't seen his mother that morning. Right away, he started praying to God it wasn't her lying there dead. "Please... Please... Please... Please... Please," he whispered rapidly.

Although her skin had become greenish-blue in color, with her face exposed, he recognized her. "Oh my God." It was Jennifer Nocks. Dillon was petrified, yet at the same time relieved it wasn't his mother. He stood up straight, wiping the blood from his hands onto his 'this buds for you' cannabis monogrammed t-shirt. But unable to keep his composure, he doubled over, puking his guts out as the stench of her rotting body paired with the realization that he'd just found a dead corpse overwhelmed him. He had to get out of there. Dillon wiped his forearm across his mouth, cleaning it as best as he could as he sprinted off through the woods in search for help.

It wasn't long before the woods were swarming with law enforcement. The area around her body had been sectioned off with yellow crime scene tape. They were dusting for prints and gathering what evidence they could find from the crime scene. One officer took pictures of Jennifer's corps, while another with gloved hands, picked up the bloody boulder used to smash in her skull, bagging it as evidence. Dillon stood there silent, nerves on edge with his arms folded tight as Detective O'Connell questioned him.

"So, when was the last time you saw her alive?"

He started to sweat, as the detective's question had caused him to be even more nervous.

"At the party I had the night before last. I remember... She was wearing those same clothes."

"What time did she leave? Did she leave alone?"

Dillon searched his mind, hoping for a mental picture of what Jennifer was doing that night, even though he was pretty hammered. "I don't know. I was kinda out of it. I do remember the party was pretty much over by the time she left."

Detective O'Connell stared Dillon in the eyes for a brief moment, looking for signs of dishonesty, before lowering his head to take down notes in his booklet. He made it a point not to grant Dillon a clue as to whether or not he believed his story.

"Did she talk to anyone?"

"Yeah... I guess," Dillon nodded his head, obnoxiously. "It was a party. Everyone was talking."

Noticing Dillon's condescending demeanor, Detective O'Connell looked up at him, taking a more austere tone. "Listen here, kid... Don't be a smart ass. Don't think I didn't catch the fact that you mentioned being pretty out of it. What were you on, drugs? Booze? You aren't twenty-one yet, and you sure as hell don't have a medical marijuana license. Don't make me haul you off to jail. Now, I'm gonna ask you again, and you better think real hard about your reply. Did she talk to anyone in particular?"

Dillon stuffed his hands in his pants pockets, then shrugged his shoulders, "Jennifer always stuck pretty close to her best friend, Shannon. You should probably ask her. She could tell you more about what Jennifer did that night than I could," he recalled in a more humbled voice.

"Last time I'm gonna say it. I'm questioning you right now, so I suggest you think hard, kid."

Dillon swallowed, but because his mouth was still dry from having smoked marijuana that morning, it felt as if a lump had formed in his throat. He reflected a brief moment upon Detective O'Connell's previous question. Suddenly, his eyebrows raised as something had come to mind. "I remember," he said, removing one hand from the pocket of his jeans, before raking it through his hair, then giving it a little tug to assist him in recollection of the scenario. "Yeah, she was talking to this guy named Jeff, before she left. He's the school mascot."

"Did they argue?"

"No. Everything looked fine to me."

"Was there tension between her and any of the other guests at the party?"

"Not that I noticed. Everything was fine. The party was chill."

Detective O'Connell glanced down at Dillon's t-shirt.

"What is that, grits?"

"I had grits for breakfast," Dillon admitted, looking down at the vomit that had soaked into his clothing.

Detective O'Connell pointed over at the vomit on the leaves, "I take it that's your mess? Looks like more than grits to me. Clean yourself up, kid."

Having gotten as much information as he felt Dillon could offer at that point, Detective O'Connell held out his card. "Okay, thanks for your help. Give me a call me if you remember anything else."

Dillon felt downtrodden, but at the same time relieved that the questioning was finally over. He took the card, stuffing it in his back pocket, before taking off. Detective O'Connell watched him as he walked away, noticing his slumped shoulders. It was evident that the questioning had taken a lot out of him.

"Hey, kid," Detective O'Connell called out to him.

Dillon dreaded what was to come. He stopped, then turned back, making eye contact with Detective O'Connell.

"Don't tell anyone about this."

That's it? Thank God, he thought. "I just want to forget it. Trust me," he nodded, assuredly.

Detective O'Connell peered over at Jennifer's corpse. Although always inclined to do his duty, he was not at all looking forward to notifying her parents that their daughter had been murdered.

Meanwhile, Shawn had just come into the house, and like most teen boys his age, he darted straight for the kitchen. Starved, he raided the refrigerator, grabbing a piece of chicken. Leftovers from one of the many dinners, he and Megan had neglected to eat together. Shawn chomped down on the drumstick, bobbing his head in acknowledgment of its deliciousness. On autopilot, he strolled into the living room to check the answering machine. "You have one new message."

"Hi Mrs. Slater, this is Mrs. Schwartz. We really need to discuss some things regarding your son, Shawn. Please give me a call as soon as you get this. My number is 555-2800." BEEP

Shawn's chewing had stopped, abruptly, as he stood there feeling less than pleased. "What ever happened to doctor patient confidentiality?"

He mashed a button on the machine, deleting Linda's message. "Bitch." Shawn wasn't looking forward to dealing with his parents' reaction to what he'd ranted about in his last therapy session with Linda.

DING DONG DING DONG, the door bell chimed. Shawn moved toward the front door, lacking any reminisces of urgency as Dillon pounded on the door. BOOM! BOOM!BOOM!

"I'm coming!! Chill out!!" Finally Shawn reached the front door. "Who is it?"

"Dude, open the door! It's Dillon," he shouted, while attempting to peek through a small rectangle of stained glass on the front door.

As Shawn opened the door, Dillon rushed in sweating and panting, as if he'd just run a marathon.

"Dude, what's wrong with you? And, what the hell is that on your shirt?"

Dillon bent over, resting a hand on his knee as he held the other one up toward Shawn, halting further questions until he could catch his breath. Once composed enough to speak, Dillon started in. "You won't believe this, man. Okay, so I'm cutting through the woods behind my house... Just walking along, rocking out... playing some air guitar. Next thing I know... I'm tripping over a dead body. It was Jennifer Nocks, man. She's dead, dude."

"This is her blood," he revealed, pointing to his shirt.

Shawn looked down at Dillon's shirt, then back up at him with a skeptical expression. "Really? Blood?"

"Dude it's blood, man. I mean... Well, it's grits... and some other stuff too, but I threw up when I saw her all dead and shit," Dillon explained, trying to convince him.

Shawn raised his eyebrows, causing his forehead to wrinkle, "Whatever you say, dude."

Dillon felt as though he had to procure Shawn's empathy, as far as why he'd lost his stomach. "I mean... Come on... It was a dead body. It fucking grossed me out."

Shawn bit into his chicken, brushing off Dillon's story. "Did your step-dad get a new batch of something?" Shawn shook his head, as if he were disappointed. "Dude... I'll admit, most of the shenanigans you pull are pretty funny, but I've gotta tell ya this one's kinda sick. You're starting to worry me."

Dillon grabbed hold to Shawn's shirt, clutching it tight as he stared him directly in the eyes. "No dude... I'm serious. I haven't even smoked that much today."

"Seriously?"

Dillon nodded affirming its truth, "Seriously, Shawn..."

As Dillon witnessed Shawn's facial expression slowly transition from disbelief to an actual realization of what he'd just told him to be true, he released Shawn's shirt from his clutches.

Shawn was at a loss for words as he walked into the living room, with Dillon slowly trailing behind. He plopped down on the couch, however, the look on his face left a bit to be desired. After Sam was murdered, he'd learned to somewhat harden himself. "Damn... that's..." He paused, not sure how to react. "Dude, what the fuck is going on here?"

The Nocks' family home was easily the most extravagant in their town, thanks to Jennifer's father. Mr. Nocks was a middle aged plastic surgeon. But, his practice was located in Los Angeles, California, which meant he was out of town more often than not. Mrs. Nocks was a stay at home mother, and nearly ten years younger than her husband. She busied herself maintaining their beautiful home, with the help of a few service staff, of course. In her spare time, she enlisted the support of the other women in the area to join her in participating in the long time tradition of pageantry, for the girls in and around Crimson County. Mrs. Nocks was a former pageant queen, but once she and Mr. Nocks were married, she gladly hung up her crown to be a mother. Jennifer was their only child, and Mrs. Nocks' pride and joy. She'd participated in and won over twenty pageants. Jennifer could get whatever she wanted, whenever she wanted, as far as Mrs. Nocks was concerned. Mr. Nocks, however, was far more strict on his contemptuous, entitled daughter. In fact, in recent months, he'd found out Jennifer was dating a much older man, and repossessed her pearl white Audi convertible because of the relationship, which is precisely why she was walking home the night she'd been slain.

That afternoon Mrs. Nocks was at home. It was an off day for the service staff, so she had the duty of watering the plants, tidying the house and finishing up their laundry. She always believed that if you looked good, you'll feel good. And although she was wearing an apron over her attire, she looked flawless, even as she cleaned her home. Her black eyeliner perfectly showcased the inner calm in her stone gray eyes. Her long, thick, jet black hair was pinned up into a bun, which helped her to complete her tasks with calm and grace. Like a true pageant queen at heart, she wore a sleeveless, pastel green, ruffle pleated chiffon dress, which came just a few inches above the knee. It matched her pastel green, Mary Jane high heels perfectly. She hadn't a care in the world as she stood in the laundry room folding her delicate undergarments one by one, neatly adding each one to the stacked pile.

In the woods nearby, the authorities had just finished up gathering what evidence they could to help them with the investigation of Jennifer's murder. Her body had already been carted off to the hospital morgue, where her parents would be required to come to identify her body. Detective O'Connell stood alone in the woods as the last of the deputies left the seen. He anguished over how he'd break the news of Jennifer's murder to her parents. Normally that was a duty Sheriff Laskey would take on. It would be Detective O'Connell's first time.

Their small town wasn't accustomed to the crime of murder. Unfortunately, they'd been seemingly struck with that plague within the past year, which is why he'd never been obligated to inform a loved one about a death in the family. Nevertheless, as an officer of the law, he knew it was something he'd signed up for.

The detective made his way back through the brush, in turmoil over what he'd say. With his car parked not far from there, and the Nocks' residence just a couple of blocks away, it felt as if the time he had left was drifting fast, like sand through an hourglass. His chest seemed to become more and more constricted with every fleeting minute. Once he'd gotten into his squad car, he took deep breaths, exhaling slowly each time, as a way of relieving the tension. After a few minutes, Detective O'Connell started his vehicle, then headed to the Nocks' home. On the short drive there he'd decided against actually saying the words, your daughter was found dead. He would more or less allow them to come to that conclusion, while revealing as little information as he possibly could. Just as the

O'Connell got out of his vehicle, a female officer pulled up behind him, hopping out of her squad car, "I figured you'd need some help breaking the news," the officer suggested as she headed his way. Thank God, he thought.

"It would be greatly appreciated," he expressed graciously.

"No problem."

The female officer knew how emotionally draining it could be informing a loved one of a death in their family. Being sure to show empathy, yet at the same time finding the right words to say to provide them comfort, was too much for one person to bare. Not to mention, the task of having to deal with their reaction. The officers were going in blind.

As the two of them walked up the long, black, cobble stone, paved driveway to the house, the female officer's appreciative gaze wandered over the property. The American flag that waved in the wind against the picturesque blue sky near the roof of their home was as large as a king sized bed sheet. The female officer peered up in awe of the tall marble pillars along each side of the porch as Detective O'Connell pressed the door bell.

Once the door bell chimed, Mrs. Nocks had already grabbed a porcelain vase to fill with water. It would hold the fresh yellow tulips she'd just clipped. She made her way carefully down the winding staircase with the vase wrapped in her right arm and nestled closely to her breast. When she'd made it across the foyer, she straightened her apron before opening the door. A wry grin formed upon her face when she saw the officers at her door step. "Ohhh, well hello, officers... How can I help you?" she inquired with a tinge of worry in her voice.

Detective O'Connell was frozen. He couldn't bear to break the news to her. The female officer had almost immediately taken notice to his hesitation, prompting her to take the lead.

"Mrs. Nocks, I presume?"

"Yes. I'm Mrs. Nocks. Is there something wrong, officers?"

"Mrs. Nocks... I'm very sorry to have to inform you."

"Inform me of what," Mrs. Nocks interrupted, already in agony over their presence at her door step. She knew something had happened to either her husband or daughter.

"We're here regarding your daughter, Jennifer."

"Oh my God! Is she okay? Is she..." Mrs. Nocks paused, not allowing herself to ask if her daughter was dead.

Detective O'Connell finally managed to speak, "We're very sorry, Mrs. Nocks."

Mrs. Nocks' eyes gazed over. The devastation she felt was more than she could take. Before they could catch her, Mrs. Nocks' body had dropped simultaneously with the porcelain vase, crashing against the granite floor.

E. RAYE TURONEK

8

Monday morning at Long Lake High looked to be the usual seen. The initial bell sounded, signaling the start of the school day as students continued pouring into the front entrance. Naturally, some were just pulling into the parking lot, having gotten a late start that morning. Still, nothing was out of the ordinary. The halls were bustling with sounds. Along with the shuffling of feet, and students fiddling with their lockers, there was an abundance of chatter to be heard as well. Most students conversed about how their weekends fared as members of the faculty stood watch in the halls, urging students to get to their classes on time. However, none of the gossip being spilled detailed the weekends' tragic events. Not a single soul looked to be mourning the death of their fellow comrade. With Crimson being such a small town you'd think that Jennifer's brutal murder would be the topic of discussion amongst the students. It was apparent that the sheriff's office was doing the best they could to overt widespread panic among the towns people, as they feared news of Jennifer's death would do just that.

Inside, upperclassmen streamed through senior hall, making their way to their assigned homerooms, before the tardy bell rang. Dillon caught a glimpse of Shawn through the downpour of teens, not too far from him, retrieving text books from his locker.

He figured that by the time he could make it through the crowd, Shawn would already be gone. In order to get his attention, Dillon threw his arms in the air as he called out to him. "Hey Shawn, wait up!"

Shawn closed his locker, but lingered there a few seconds, giving Dillon enough time to nudge his way through the crowd. Once Dillon caught up, the pair took off together.

"What's up with the shades, man? The sun isn't even out yet."

"I had a late night."

Shawn grinned, "I bet."

"Dude, you got any candy?"

Shawn studied Dillon, suspicious as to why he was craving candy so early in the morning.

"Dude, are you stoned?" Shawn guessed.

Dillon shrugged his shoulders as a gesture of affirmation to his question.

"Come on, man. It's eight o'clock in the morning. Don't you think you should tone it down?"

"I know, but ever since I found Jennifer's dead body in the woods with her head all bashed in, I haven't been able to get the image out of my head," Dillon uttered quietly, so none of the other students passing by could hear. I just needed to relax, man. My mom's Xanax wasn't working, so I did what came natural."

He quivered, chasing the disconcerting image from his thoughts, then immediately, something caught his eye.

There was a snack stand set up in the hallway, fundraising for the upcoming senior trip. Two fellow stoners, Stacy and Kelly, were working the stand. Dillon was almost as fond of Stacy, as much as he was marijuana. He'd always been intrigued by her Gothic rocker panache. Kelly also shared his flair for odd piercings, dark eye shadow, black skinny jeans and tight black shorts. However, because of her droopy chin and muffin top shaped torso, her suitors were few and far between.

Snacks and Stacy, the combination was too enticing to ignore. "Dude," he nudged Shawn with his elbow, attempting to inconspicuously alert him of Stacy's presence. "Stacy's working the snack stand. I'll catch you later." Dillon was drawn her way.

Shawn shook his head, disapproving of Dillon's moronic demeanor. "Later, dude," he mumbled as he made a swift left turn to travel down the hall where Mrs. Schwartz's office could be found. When Shawn came upon her door he tried turning the knob, but it was locked. Shawn peered through the glass on the door, noticing that the lights were still out.

Out of nowhere, Mr. Ramsey, the senior counselor walked up behind him. "If you're looking for Mrs. Schwartz, she hasn't made it in yet." Shawn turned his attention to Mr. Ramsey. "In fact, if you don't make it to homeroom in about thirty seconds, you're gonna be in the same boat, buddy."

Shawn's eyes grew wide, "Oh no," he exclaimed sarcastically, before quickly switching his demeanor, throwing up his hands, "I'm kidding... No need to alert the authorities. I'm going." Shawn walked off, just as the tardy bell sounded.

"Last semester Joe... You can do it," he encouraged himself, in dire need of a short pep talk to commence his day. It had become very clear to him, while being a counselor at Long Lake High over the past four years, that the majority of the upperclassmen there were spoiled, disrespectful, and unappreciative.

In homeroom, Emma sat in silence, looking fixedly down at her text book, focused on her studies. Or so it seemed to those around her. She was actually wondering why Shawn hadn't made it to class yet. It wasn't like him to be late. I hope everything is okay, she thought. Although he didn't speak about it, she was aware that the anniversary of his sister's death had just passed, and remained worried about how it would affect him.

A moment later, Shawn entered the classroom. "Nice of you to join us, Shawn," the teacher, Mrs. Kneely, pointed out as she gathered her notes from her desk for the morning lesson.

Emma looked up, gazing upon him. Her heart instantly began pounding, watching his every movement as he made his way to his seat. Sure enough, Shawn glanced her way. To her, his feelings were evident, however, his look of adornment for her went unnoticed among their fellow classmates. Not that they would take notice, anyway. Most of them were attempting to communicate with one another inconspicuously, or engaged in text messaging with their cell phones while their text books sat on the desktops in front of them, ignored.

Mrs. Kneely stood wearily, writing the day's lesson on the chalkboard. Sadly, writing just one sentence took her quite some time. She'd grown tired over the course of her fifty-year career, there at Long Lake High. Her husband was deceased, which made her reluctant to retire, for fear of being alone and growing senile.

The board read: *Murder's out of tune and sweet revenge grows harsh. Othello*

Finally, she turned to the class. "Can anyone tell me what Othello meant by this?"

She gestured toward the board, with her pointing stick, reading aloud, "Murders out of tune and sweet revenge grows harsh."

No one answered. All communication seemed to cease. One could say, it had become so quiet you could hear a pin drop. The students looked around, waiting to see which brave soul would dare to answer her query. All the while, Mrs. Kneely eyeballed Shawn. She had already set her sights on him, when he walked through the door. She felt a sort of personal disrespect whenever a student was late to her class. "Nobody? Shawn?"

Already immersed in thought of her question, he gazed as if he was somehow looking at and past her at the same time. "I think he meant that sometimes death falls upon the wrong person. But because death is certain, it eventually falls back on who it was meant, only under cruelest of circumstances."

Mrs. Kneely was surprised by his answer. Although it wasn't what she had in mind, she was still intrigued by the possibility of its truth. The majority of his classmates were left perplexed by his response.

The public announcement system chimed. Shawn snapped back to reality, his attention then turned to the speaker on the wall. A man's voice came over the public announcement speaker. "Attention students this is your principal. Please remember that the Crimson County Police Department has issued a ten o'clock curfew due to the recent string of untimely deaths throughout our community. For your own safety, please adhere to the curfew."

Displeased with the news of the extension of the early curfew, most of the students became disorderly. While some shouted, "BOOOO," as they threw balled up wads of paper at the public announcement speaker, others expressed their disapproval by simply yelling out reasons as to why they couldn't possibly be contained indoors at such an early hour.

Emma and Shawn locked eyes once more. The lack of respect she felt for her classmates, because of their shenanigans, was clearly visible once she rolled her eyes, then looked up toward the ceiling, as if to say, when will it ever end. Although Shawn shared her sentiments, he didn't expect anything less than the current reaction, knowing all to well the maturity of his peers. He casually shrugged his shoulders, along with a nod of the head.

Mrs. Kneely attempted to calm the class. As she fixed her mouth to speak, the wrinkles along the edges of her thin lips creased, her turkey neck began to wattle, finally with a trembling voice she yelled, "Settle down students."

Not wanting to cause her a heart attack, the students calmed all at once.

"This is serious. You kids need to follow this curfew until the monster committing these murders is apprehended," Mrs. Kneely uttered angrily.

Derrick, a student who prided himself on being a smart ass, raised his hand, waving it flamboyantly through the air, itching to gain her attention.

Even though Mrs. Kneely was reluctant to acknowledge him, she did anyway, giving him the benefit of the doubt, in hopes that maybe he'd back her up with a positive response, being that the situation at hand was a serious one.

"Yes, Derrick," she called out, allowing him to speak.

"Mrs. Kneely, are you gonna follow the curfew?"

Mrs. Kneely stood there silent, thinking what a mistake she'd made acknowledging him.

"You do know that means... None of those wild, late night bingo parties?" Derrick chuckled, looking left then right for validation of his humor, which was bestowed from the majority of the students as they snickered quietly, indeed finding his question amusing.

Mrs. Kneely shook her head, disappointed by their lack of

humility. "As a matter of fact, I am Derrick. It's called leading by example. Now, all of you turn your textbooks to page one twenty seven, or do you all need Derrick to do it first?"

At that point, Mrs. Kneely's nerves had begun to show. As her head twitched continuously, the students became inclined to comply, feeling she'd suffered enough aggravation.

Meanwhile, Megan had just picked up her clothing from the dry cleaners downtown. She power-walked down Main Street with a tight grip on the hangers, which held the clothing hanging over her left shoulder. She fumbled through her purse, hanging on the right, but only for a brief moment before successfully retrieving her cellular phone. When she finally had to stop at the corner because of a red light, she made her call.

"Hi, it's me. I wanted to apologize to you about the other night, but I don't want to do it over the phone. Please, just call me. I need..." Megan paused mid-sentence as something caught her eye.

It was Ron. He was having his lunch, al fresco, at a bistro on the opposite corner, and to Megan's surprise, he was with a female companion. Megan squinted to see as much as she possibly could from her vantage point, but all she could make out was that the woman was blonde, seemingly attractive, slim, and quite busty. She'd never seen her before, so she had no clue as to the woman's identity. Without completing her message, Megan disconnected her call. She watched intently as Ron gazed into the woman's eyes, gently caressing underneath her chin with his fingertips, only to bring her in close, before running his thumb down her lips, finally tasting them passionately.

His actions had devastated Megan, taking her breath away. It took her a moment to force back her emotions, but for fear they'd soon surface, Megan bolted in the opposite direction, colliding into the person behind her. Her dry cleaning dropped to the ground.

"I'm so sorry."

The two of them bent over simultaneously to pick up the clothing, causing them to bump heads.

"Oh, sorry," Megan apologized, holding her forehead, but finally making eye contact with the gentleman. He was attractive, but her mind was preoccupied with Ron, at the moment.

"Here let me," he insisted with a slight chuckle.

Megan stood waiting as the polite stranger gathered her belongings from the sidewalk. Meanwhile, she parceled out subtle glances at Ron, wondering if he'd noticed her there.

Ron and his female companion seemed to feed off of each others flirtatious gestures as they sipped their afternoon mojitos. It was almost enough to make Megan spontaneously gag, and she would have, had she not been in the company of a stranger.

"Thanks." She'd witnessed more than she could bare of Ron's indiscretions, so she hastily grabbed her clothing, pushing past the gentleman to continue on her way.

"Whoa... Hey," he called out to her, following in close pursuit.

Megan belted out a heavy sigh of frustration, before turning around to answer him. "Look I don't mean to be rude, but I'm..."

Sensing a let down was in progress, before he'd even had the opportunity to ask, he interrupted. "I'm sorry... I don't normally do this, but I'd be crazy not to ask, because you are drop dead gorgeous. Would you mind having lunch with me sometime?"

His compliment caused her to blush. She considered his proposal, glancing over at Ron, still immersed in deep conversation. Jealousy successfully pushed her to accept the stranger's invite. Seeing Ron there had rendered her emotionally vulnerable, or at the very least that's what her excuse would be, after she slept with him.

"Sure. Why not?"

"Great. By the way, I'm Steven," he introduced himself, flashing his pearly whites.

She smiled back softly, no doubt, unsure of whether she'd made the right decision. "I'm Megan. It's a pleasure to meet you," she replied, holding out her hand. Steven took hold to her delicate fingers, turning her hand as he lifted it to his lips. Finally, he planted a kiss on the back of her hand that tingled her to her very core.

Back at the high school the halls were virtually empty, since classes were still in session. When the bell rang signaling the end of third period, the students exited their classes, once again flooding the halls. Emma left the classroom just before Shawn. Shortly after, Shannon followed.

"Hey Shawn, wait up!" Shannon scurried toward Shawn, wrapping her book bag over her shoulder.

Shawn slowed his pace, however he avoided a complete stop, in order keep Emma from feeling jealous. Shannon caught up to Shawn, then continued walking alongside him as Emma stole peeks at the two of them from her locker, ahead.

"What's up?"

Shannon gave his arm a little nudge with her shoulder, "Are you coming to the bonfire at the pier, tonight?"

Shawn's eyebrows wrinkled. Shannon had never personally invited him to an event before. Quite frankly, he was uncomfortable even talking to her with Emma lurking close by.

"What about the curfew?"

"What about it? There's gonna be a ton of us there. Nothing bad could happen, Shawn."

Dillon ran up from behind, stuffed himself in between the two of them, then threw his arms around their shoulders. Dillon, you're a life saver, Shawn thought to himself.

He was pumped. "Dude. Shady Point Pier, tonight," he announced, with his head turned toward Shawn. Dillon then turned to look at Shannon. "Hey, Shannon," he uttered flirtatiously. She wasn't really his type at all, however, this was his way of letting her know that he was aware of her intentions to push up on Shawn.

Although Shannon found him a tad revolting, she humored him due to the fact that he was Shawn's best friend. "Dillon," she replied in the driest of tones, before rolling her eyes.

Dillon could sense the agitation in her voice, but it was a greeting none the less, so he pretended not to notice. Besides, he wasn't eager to acknowledge that Shawn was obviously about to cross over into the popular crowd, and he hadn't received the same reception. Still, Dillon fully planned on tagging along for the ride.

Shannon walked off, lifting Dillon's arm from her shoulder. "I'll see you there, Shawn."

Seeing an opportunity to brighten her mood, Shannon purposely rammed her shoulder into Emma, who by no coincidence was still standing at her locker. Emma dropped her book bag spilling her materials out onto the floor, but quickly bent over to gather up her things. Sad to say, this happened to be a regular occurrence, attributable to the fact that she was the shy quiet type. Emma exuded defenselessness, so she was looked upon by her peers as a meek and timid little girl. However, nothing could be further from the truth. She was merely quiet because she had no desire to communicate with most of her peers.

Emma felt that the majority of them were mean, selfish, rude and insecure. Picking on those different or less fortunate than they were was the only thing that provided them comfort, for the time being anyway.

"I thought you were smart. Haven't you figured out by now that it's best not to stand in my way?" Shannon had noticed Emma peeking at them as they strolled up the hall toward her, and in that short time frame, she'd come to the conclusion that Emma must have the hots for Shawn. As far as Shannon was concerned, letting Emma know where she stood was imperative.

Emma refused to dignify her question with a response, instead she continued gathering up her materials in silence.

Shannon huffed, "You'll learn," then strutted off, dialing someone on her smart phone. The line didn't ring, but went straight to an automated voice mail box. "O.m.g... Jennifer, why aren't you answering? And why aren't you at school? I bet you're off slutting with that old guy again." Shannon chuckled a bit, before quickly dropping her grin. "Anyway, the party at the pier is tonight. You'd better be there. Call me back," she said, leaving her message.

When Emma finally stood, she glanced back at Shawn, before stuffing her books into her locker. Her heart raced as the anger she felt steadily boiled to the surface. With her face hidden behind her locker door, she closed her eyes and took a deep breath, exhaling slowly to calm herself. It killed Shawn to see her treated that way, yet he knew running to her rescue would further the torture Shannon was hell bent on bestowing her.

"Dude, looks like Shannon has the hots for ya."

Shannon was the last thing on Shawn's mind, but he remained reluctant to reveal his true feelings to Dillon. They were indeed best friends, but Dillon couldn't keep his mouth shut to save own his life, so he most definitely wasn't going to trust him to keep his relationship with Emma between the three of them. "You think you can pay your step-dad's closet a visit?"

Dillon looked left then right, making sure no one was watching them. "I'm one step ahead of you, dude," he admitted while discreetly taking a small sandwich bag of marijuana from the pocket of his jeans, flashing it at Shawn.

"Sweet..."

"All right, man. I'll check you later. I've gotta get to Chemistry class." They pounded fists, before Dillon headed off.

By then, the traffic in the hall had dwindled to few and far between. Shawn rushed over to Emma, gently rubbing across the small of her back with his hand, in hopes of providing her comfort.

"She's just so hateful," Emma whispered with her head hung low.

"You know, you amaze me more and more everyday. You could have easily kicked the snot outta her, and she'd deserve every bit of it, but you refuse to let them bring you down to their level. We could all learn a lot from you."

Shawn shook his head, in awe of her benevolence.

Emma raised her head and stared at him with her beautiful, big brown eyes. "I'll be fine. Shouldn't you be leaving me to head to class."

"Not a chance. You need a break. Come on, let's get outta here."

The school day was almost complete when Principal Sobieski, a tall, serious, dark-haired polish fellow, finally emerged from his office headed straight for the secretary's desk, where Peggy sat filing her long, red, already manicured fingernails. She wasn't used to doing much work. Most of her day consisted of answering the phone and taking poorly detailed messages. Other than that, she sat chomping and popping her chewing gum, a habit that started once she quit smoking several years earlier.

"I need you to put a copy of the newsletter into each faculty member's mailbox. I also need a list of every student that was absent today, along with their parents contact information. And, can you give Mrs. Schwartz a call to find out why it is she neglected coming to work today?"

Once he'd assigned her a momentary task to keep her busy doing something that actually involved her job, he felt better about stepping out to handle other supervisory duties.

Peggy opened her desk drawer, then proceeded to rifle through tons of empty gum wrappers in search for her reading glasses. "Uh... I knew they were in here somewhere." Once she got them on, she flipped through the Rolodex on her desk for Mrs. Schwartz's number.

"Ah, here we go," she declared as she'd come upon the number.

Too lazy to pick up the receiver, Peggy used the eraser end of a pencil to put the phone on speaker, before using it to dial Mrs. Schwartz's home number. The phone rang repeatedly with no answer. Peggy disconnected the call just as counselor Ramsey entered the office, arriving back from a late lunch break.

"Hey, did Mrs. Schwartz mention anything to you about taking the day off?"

A quizzical expression formed upon his face. Her inquiry concerned him, being that Mrs. Schwartz was the least irresponsible person he'd ever known. "No. She hasn't even called yet?"

"Not yet."

"Well, that's not like her at all. In fact, I'd go as far as saying, it's completely out of character for her to not call or show up. Something had to have happened."

Later that evening, the authorities were swarming in and around Linda's home, having been tipped off by the school faculty. Like any other crime scene they were busy dusting for prints, taking photographs and gathering what evidence they could to assist them in their investigation. One officer took pictures of the blood splatter on the wall, and floor of the foyer. With gloved hands, a second officer picked up the bottom half of the dead cat, bagging it as evidence. He was finding it difficult to understand why the cat had to be killed, and at the same time, disgusted by the manner in which the execution was carried out.

"What the hell?" He looked up at the other officer, "Call me pessimistic, but I'm pretty sure this counts as the ninth life."

"Ugh," the other officer initially winced, but within seconds tilted his head, giving a little nod to affirm the first officer's witty comment, after having contemplated it.

Upstairs in Linda's bedroom, Detective O'Connell took notes in an effort to access the scene. Linda's body was splayed across the bed, very dead. The phone was on the nightstand in its original positioning. Yet, the closet door was still open, showcasing her disheveled wardrobe.

Sheriff Laskey was careful as headed up the stairs, around the bloody footprints, then into Linda's bedroom. Naturally, the first thing he'd noticed was Linda's body sprawled across the bed.

"Oh, God," Sheriff Laskey blurted, bowing his head, before resting his hands upon his hips. It saddened his heart so much, that it was necessary for him to take his eyes off of her for at least a brief moment, in order to compose himself.

"Because she was the psychiatrist over at the high school, we were alerted much sooner. Her co-workers got worried when she was a no call, no show," Detective O'Connell explained.

"I just don't know if this town will ever recover, even after this animal is brought to justice."

"This just doesn't make any sense."

"None of these murders make any sense, Detective," Sheriff Laskey uttered, angrily.

Detective O'Connell took note of his frustration, therefore feeling the need to explain his take on things. "No, I mean something's off about the crime scene. I'm assuming he came out of the closet and attacked her up here. But, there was also a struggle downstairs. So, why would she come back up here instead of going out the front door?"

In deep contemplation, Sheriff Laskey moved to the stairs as Detective O'Connell followed closely. Both studied the bloody footprints in an attempt to come up with a plausible scenario.

All of a sudden, Sheriff Laskey noticed something. "There's only one pair of bloody footprints going up the stairs, which happen to be shoe-prints. Linda isn't wearing any shoes."

The two of them moved back to Linda's bedroom.

"So, whoever murdered her must have carried her body back upstairs, placing her that way purposely," Detective O'Connell continued.

"Whoever did this is on a full blown killing spree. We've got to catch em' and fast, before they strike again. Have you found any leads on social media that would help us figure out who could have possibly had it out for the Nocks girl?"

"Not yet Sheriff, but I've got several of officers combing through the students' social media accounts. It's like a computerized almanac. Those kids post every event in their entire lives on the web."

"Which is exactly what we need. See if Principal Sobieski can give us a list of all of the students Mrs. Schwartz was evaluating. And, I noticed that she's wearing a wedding band, so let's find the husband."

"I'm on it." Detective O'Connell left the room, post haste.

Sheriff Laskey stood there staring at Linda's body. "Damn!" he exclaimed, feeling downtrodden by the lack of help he and his department had been to the residents in Crimson, since the murders began. Although there was no way he could have predicted Linda would've been targeted, the feeling that he'd failed her, as well as his entire community, still weighed heavily on his conscience.

Across town, everything was quiet on the residential front, due to the fact that most of the upperclassmen were gathered at Shady Point Pier. Almost every officer on the police force was on duty, either assisting in the investigation at Linda's house or patrolling the neighborhoods. With no regard to having school the following day, the teens were spending their night swimming, listening to music, drinking beers, and getting high.

A small bonfire was lit on the sand where Shawn sat, all by his lonesome, watching everyone else busy doing whatever it was that amused them. Shawn had only come to the party because it allowed him the opportunity to avoid his mother.

Shannon was buzzed and on the prowl, no doubt. She could be seen prancing up the beach from one group of individuals to the next, chatting it up as she made her way toward Shawn. Soon she was walking over to him carrying two opened beers, she'd finagled from a couple of gullible guys who were hoping to get laid that night.

"Shawn, you came. Want a beer?"

"Of course... Who'd turn down free beer?" he responded graciously.

Shannon saw that as an invitation to join him, so she handed him one of the beers then plopped down next to him. "I told you there were gonna be a lot of people here. I'm glad that you decided to come. Ya know, with the rash of murders and all, my mom has been freaking out. I can barely leave the house to go to school."

"Yeah, mine too. Then again, my mom has been like that since my uh..." Shawn paused, abandoning that train of thought, realizing she could care less about his sister. She and Jennifer were supposed to be the best of friends, and she hadn't a clue what happened to her yet. She probably hasn't even tried to find out, he thought. "It's been a while now," he continued.

She knew exactly what he'd neglected to say. "Oh yeah, I remember you're sister. She was..." Shannon hesitated, attempting to think of something nice to say. "Quiet. She would have graduated last year. I can't imagine how much you must miss her. You guys were pretty close, right?"

Once again, right on time, Dillon walked up shifting Shawn's attention from Shannon. He stood there with his arms sprawled out, welcoming them. "Shawn. Shannon. You crazy kids... I got the reefer who wants to chief?"

Neither of them could get a word out before Dillon was already pulling a joint from the breast pocket of his flannel shirt, taking a seat on the sand, Indian style, right next to Shawn, and lighting up the joint.

Shawn grinned, giving him a fist bump. "What's up, dude? Glad to see you finally made it."

Dillon puffed the joint, "I wouldn't miss it, if my life depended on it," he said while holding in the smoke, before hurriedly blowing it back out, in a chuckle, "And it just might."

"Dude, I swear some of the shit that comes out of your mouth..." Shawn shook his head in discord, "Give me the joint, dude."

Dillon passed the joint over to Shawn. "I only speak the truth, man. The truth, and nothing but the truth," he quoted with his shoulders raised. Then dropping his shoulders, he raised his chin as he turned his attention to Shannon. "What's up on the beers, Shannon?"

Even though Shannon thought that Dillon was a grade-A douchebag, she could bare him long enough to smoke up his marijuana. Therefore, she had no objections to fetching him a beer. "I'll get you one."

Shannon hurried off while Dillon gawked at her buttocks,

which was being showcased in a tight-fitting blue jean mini-skirt.

Shawn continued smoking, taking a few more puffs than he normally would. With Sam on his mind his mood had turned sour, however not being the most intuitive person, Dillon hadn't even noticed.

"Thank God for parents born in the sixties. Dude, I got twenty bucks that says, you're hitting that tonight."

Shawn exhaled, passing the joint back to Dillon.

"What are you talking about, man?"

"Shannon. You know she's asking for it."

Before Shawn could reply, Shannon returned, handing over a beer to Dillon, who reciprocated her kindness by passing her the joint. "Thank you," she exclaimed with a generous amount of exaggeration.

As she took a drag, Derrick walked up behind her, and in an attempt at coming off smooth and flirtatious, he poked her in the side, catching her by surprise, "Boo."

"Ahh!" Startled, Shannon jerked away, turning fast to see who was behind her.

Once she'd seen that it was Derrick, a glimmer of surprise flashed across her face, before she gave one of his nipples the old pinch and twist. "How does that feel? Boo..."

"Alright... Alright... What do ya say, we call it a truce?"

She was as fond of him as he was her, however this way she got a free feel, while creating the illusion for Shawn that she was attempting to cause Derrick some discomfort. She didn't want to come off as being easy. Even though that was precisely the case. Shawn was well aware of what was going on, and he couldn't care less either way. As far as he was concerned, he was spoken for. Besides, the talk of Sam had ruined his night altogether.

Derrick slowly took her hand, "Come here... I wanna show you something." Shannon closed her eyes, catching her bottom lip with her teeth. "Mmm... This should be good."

Shannon passed the joint back to Dillon as Derrick pulled her away. "I'll be right back, guys. Save me some."

"Dude, what a cock blocker." Dillon was disappointed, having missed an opportunity to live vicariously through Shawn. "I got twenty bucks that says, he's hitting that tonight."

Shawn couldn't resist. He looked toward Dillon, flashing him a slight grin, a little amused by his stupidity. At which point, they both began to chuckle. Although being a friend of Dillon's came with the luxury of free marijuana, his carefree personality was actually the main reason Shawn enjoyed being in his company so often. Dillon carried on, imitating Shannon's voice, "I'll be right back, guys," he joked, before turning his fist to the side, motioning it back and forth toward his mouth, while at the same time, forcing his tongue to bulge from the side of his cheek.

"Dude, she's so not hitting this shit when she comes back,"

he assured Shawn, before puffing the joint.

After a few hours midnight had rolled around, and most of the teens were still partying at the Pier, with the exception of only a few people.

Derrick and Shannon emerged from the lake, ending their late night dip. Although they were dressed in the appropriate swimwear, the temperature had dropped nearly ten degrees, which caused the them to shutter as they were hit by gusts of the night's cool breeze. The two tip-toed quickly through the sand, at last, grabbing towels off of the beach for cover. "Let's go to my car and get warmed up."

Shannon shivered, cloaked in her towel, "Uhhh... that sounds great."

"It has gotten really nippy out," she complained as they scurried off to Derrick's car, both intent on doing more than just warming up. Once they got inside, he locked the doors, and with little to no hesitation the two locked lips. Derrick began to climb on top of her, but the center console made it difficult for their make out session to flow smoothly. Determined to steady the mood, he kissed her down the side of her neck. "The back seat," she suggested, giving him a more comfortable option.

He smiled, backing off, "You first." Shannon climbed into the back, encouraged by a spank on her behind. "Naughty girl..." Derrick followed, immediately climbing on top of her.

A masked assailant emerged from the woods nearby. He was dressed in all black and toting a black duffel bag. As he moved surreptitiously toward Derrick's car, he crouched down low, which allowed him to remain unnoticed. The assailant crept around the vehicle, sticking metal stakes he'd pulled from his bag deep into the grass, alongside each door on the vehicle.

Still in the throws of passion, Derrick and Shannon neglected to notice the assailant as he poured gasoline onto the roof of the car. The liquid quickly flowed down the windows and body of the vehicle. The stranger continued by pouring a trail, which led back to the edge of the woods.

Finally, the assailant lit a match, igniting the trail of gasoline. Fire raced toward the vehicle, engulfing it in flames.

The first of the teens to notice the flames had begun to point and holler out, alerting others of the fire. Everyone ran toward the car, yet no-one dared to get too close. Most of them were so inebriated that they thought it was some sort of prank, and cheered on the mischief. "Woooo whoo! Yeah!" Only a select few knew better.

"What the fuck?!" Derrick and Shannon hollered out in a panic, tugging on the door handles. But they were locked, thanks to Derrick. He hopped into the driver's seat to unlock the doors as Shannon pounded hysterically on the windows. They both tugged mercilessly at the handles, slamming their shoulders against the doors. But to no avail, because although Derrick had unlocked them, the metal stakes were preventing the doors from budging even in the slightest. Their screams were simultaneous. "What the fuck?! Help us! Somebody Help!"

Kelly yelled out, "What the hell is going on?!"

A friend of Derrick's noticed the vehicle, "Dude, that's Derrick's car!"

Kelly became horrified, once she'd caught a glimpse of movement inside of the burning vehicle. "Oh my God! Is somebody in there?! I think somebody's in there!"

BOOM!!! The car exploded, lifting it several feet from the ground. The impact from the blast lifted the teens off of their feet, forcing them back through the air, then dropping them onto the sand. The car came crashing down, causing a second explosion. BOOM!

For a moment, everyone was disoriented. Their ears were ringing, but all other noise seemed muffled. Once their ears began to function normally, most of the girls could be heard either sobbing or moaning in discomfort. Several of the guys struggled to their feet and began to help others from the ground.

"Is everyone okay?" One teen boy called out as he clutched his abdomen.

Derrick and Shannon never stood a chance. The initial blast had taken their lives, instantaneously.

9

The next day, school had been canceled due the horrifying events that took place at Shady Pointe Pier the night prior. However, that evening students and staff gathered together in the schoolyard to pay their respects. A candlelight vigil was being held in memory of those that had tragically lost their lives. There were flowers placed all around the photographs of those who'd been murdered. Even a photo of Jennifer was there among the others. The news of her murder had spread after the incident at the pier. The sheriff's department decided that it was no longer necessary to keep her death quiet, due to the rapid rate at which individuals were being targeted. The authorities cautioned everyone to be aware and on guard at all times.

Students humbly approached the photos, leaving flowers, teddy bears, and other personal artifacts in tribute to their fallen peers. Most stood there sobbing as they comforted one another. Dillon wrapped his arms around Stacy as she wept.

Vigil or no vigil, there was no way Shawn was getting out of the house as far as Megan was concerned. Especially after she'd found out about him being at the pier that fateful night.

Once the vigil was nearly over and most had already left the schoolyard, only a few cars remained in the parking lot, one of which belonged to Emma. Emma had attended the candlelight vigil due to her great admiration for Mrs. Schwartz. She felt compelled to pay her respects. After all,

Mrs. Schwartz had counseled her on many occasions. She'd assisted her in healing many of the emotional wounds she bared because of her peers malicious behavior.

As Emma headed toward her vehicle, she realized that not only was it dark out, but she'd also parked at the end of the lot. With all that had happened fresh on her mind, Emma was cautious as she hurried along her way.

Halfway there she heard footsteps, and without hesitation, turned to see who was there.

"Hey! Who's there?" The footsteps stopped and Emma didn't see anyone, so she kept moving. A few seconds later, she heard something else. When Emma turned around that time, there was an empty soda can rolling across the parking lot, clanking as it was carried across the cement by gusts of wind. Still there was no one there.

Emma wasn't as scared as most would be in this predicament, due to the fact that she'd been the butt of many pranks pulled by her classmates. This could very well be another one of their sick games, she thought. Although pulling a prank on her at a time of such turmoil would be in poor taste, she'd learned the hard way not to put anything past her peers. Nevertheless, if indeed it happened to be someone who meant to cause her physical harm, she was prepared for that as well. Emma sped up her pace, yet kept her head high as she grabbed something from her purse. She wanted to be sure her hair didn't drape over the sides of her face, covering her peripheral sights.

Just as she passed one of the cars in the parking lot a

masked assailant grabbed her from behind, wrapping one arm tight around her neck, then covered her mouth with the opposite hand. Emma reacted in an instant, spraying the assailant in the face with pepper spray. "Ahhh!" The attacker hollered in pain from the sting of the spray. He released her, rubbing his eyes in a panic. Emma turned to him, took a step back like a football kicker, then snapped her right foot backward, before launching it forward into his groin. "How's that, you fucker?!" His breath was taken away as he bent over in agony, clutching his groin. Emma grabbed his head, slamming her knee into his face. The assailant collapsed to the ground, holding tight to his mask, so that she couldn't pull it off. Finally, Emma sent her foot crashing down on his leg once, twice, then again a third time.

"Ahhh! Fuck!" he hollered out, using his hands to shield his leg in an attempt to cushion further blows, "You, little bitch!"

"Looks like you picked the wrong bitch this time, you pussy."

Emma had strong legs. She thought for sure that once he got up, he'd be limping. It was her chance. Emma bolted to her car, but fumbled through her purse for the keys, dropping them in a panic. "Shit."

She quickly glanced back, finding the assailant was still there on the ground, so she crouched to her knees, then reached out to retrieve her keys from under her vehicle. "Got 'em."

Hopping to her feet, she turned right away to check for him. Her attacker had vanished. She squinted her eyes, scanning the entire area around her, but she didn't see him. Again, Emma fumbled with her keys a few seconds, before snagging the right one and opening her car door. In seconds, she'd gotten in, locked the doors and started her car. Emma sped off uncertain about what had just occurred. She wondered whether she'd really been attacked or if it were just a cruel prank.

The next morning school had resumed as usual. As expected, the halls were quiet because classes were still in session, however something was different. The atmosphere was dreadfully gloomy that day. The normal satire that flowed throughout the school amongst the students and staff had come to a halt. Once many of the upperclassmen had witnessed the murder of two of their fellow students with their own eyes, the situation that they, themselves, and the rest of the town faced had become a reality.

Because every single person that was murdered had some affiliation with Long Lake High School, Sheriff Laskey and Detective O'Connell had come up with a plan. They'd set up shop in Linda's office where they'll be conducting interviews, on an individual basis, with the students she'd been helping that school year. Sheriff Laskey would be seated behind her desk asking all the questions, while Detective O'Connell would walk back and fourth behind the students. In doing so, they were hoping to cause whomever was being interviewed to feel cornered, subsequently making them more forthcoming, as they'll want to get the interview over with as quickly as possible.

When Shawn entered the room, Sheriff Laskey immediately recognized him. "Shawn Slater, right?" He felt a great deal of pity for Shawn, because of Samantha's death.

"Last time I checked."

Shawn was already uncomfortable when it came to answering questions about his life, now his distress was compounded, because the questions were being asked in a place which caused him great agitation. But at the same time, it was difficult for him to take the authorities seriously, being that they had yet to solve his sister's murder.

"Well... have a seat, son," the sheriff instructed, noticing his hesitation.

Detective O'Connell pulled back the chair opposite Sheriff Laskey, gesturing Shawn to have a seat there.

"So how long have you been a patient of Mrs. Schwartz?"

"It's been about a year now."

Sheriff Laskey jotted something on his notepad. "One year, huh?"

"Yeah, when my sister was killed about a year ago. You guys remember my sister, right?" Shawn paused briefly, but didn't get a reply, due to the fact that his attitude change had caught Sheriff Laskey off guard. Shawn continued on with his explanation, feeling he had the upper hand.

"Well anyway, my parents thought it would be a good idea

for me to see a psychiatrist. A precaution, you know? So that I wouldn't go nuts."

Sheriff Laskey wasn't going to let Shawn patronize him. He'd decided to acknowledge his question. After all, if he expected Shawn to answer his questions honestly and give him the respect he was due, he'd have to render Shawn the same consideration. "Yes, I recognized you when you came in. You're John Slater's son."

Shawn nodded his head in affirmation.

"And to answer your question... Yes, I remember your sister. I don't think there's any way we could forget. I'm very sorry about what happened her. We're actively working on finding Samantha's killer. We think it could be the same person who killed Mrs. Schwartz. We just need to ask you a few routine questions. You know... gather as much information as we can. It's standard procedure."

"No problem."

"When was the last time you saw Mrs. Schwartz?"

"I had a session with her a couple days ago."

Sheriff Laskey looked up at Detective O'Connell. "Can you get that tape for me, Detective?"

"Sure thing, Sheriff."

Shawn looked confused as the detective left the room. "Tape... What tape?"

"Mrs. Schwartz taped all of her sessions."

"Okay, but what about doctor-patient confidentiality?"

By that time, Detective O'Connell had arrived back, tape in hand. "Here you go, Sheriff."

Detective O'Connell watched Shawn's reaction as he handed the tape over to Sheriff Laskey. Shawn was less than pleased, however he does nothing to stop the obvious infringement on his privacy.

"Thank you, Detective."

Sheriff Laskey stared Shawn in the eyes, "You know, we can't listen to the tape if you refuse us?"

Shawn took a brief moment to decide, replaying in his head the little meltdown he had in regards to his family, at he and Mrs. Schwartz's last session.

The sheriff didn't want to give him too much time to decide, so he figured he'd apply some pressure to rush Shawn along. "You don't have anything to hide. Do you?"

"No Sheriff, I don't." He didn't want his mother of all people to hear what he really thought of her, but on the other hand, Shawn also didn't want Sheriff Laskey to think he was trying to hinder the investigation.

"Good."

To ensure Shawn didn't have time to back out, Sheriff Laskey slapped an official looking document on the desk in front of him. "Here's the release form. Just sign by the X."

Shawn stalled, looking over the form as he tried to come up

with a way to keep his parents from finding out about the contents of the tape. He was sure that once the police heard what he said, not only would it be brought to his parents' attention, but his mother's affair would also become public knowledge. A fact which could be disastrous to their family's reputation.

"I don't have a pen."

"Not a problem. I always keep one handy." The sheriff pulled a pen from his shirt's breast pocket, then handed it over to Shawn. Although reluctant, he signed the release form, trying to play it cool. It was too late though, Sheriff Laskey and Detective O'Connell locked eyes as Shawn's hesitation became evident to them both. Their suspicions had been raised.

"You seem a little nervous, Shawn."

"I'm not nervous. I just like my privacy, and Mrs. Schwartz was the only person I talked to about my personal feelings."

"So you felt pretty comfortable with her?"

"No. Not really, but I'm not really comfortable with anyone."

"That doesn't make any sense. Then why is it you felt you were able to discuss your personal feelings with her?"

Detective O'Connell sat on the desk, then leaned in toward Shawn, anticipating his reply.

Shawn looked over at Detective O'Connell, "Okay," he

mumbled, wrinkling his eyebrows, before turning his focus back to Sheriff Laskey. "Look... If I didn't give her something to go on, my parents would have me in therapy my entire senior year."

Shawn's argument was convincing enough. Detective O'Connell leaned back, satisfied with his answer.

"Had she ever revealed anything to you about herself?"

"Like what?"

"You know... personal stuff."

"Well, she had some unresolved issues with her husband. He was pretty abusive, so they weren't together anymore. There is one session in particular that comes to mind. Mrs. Schwartz came in wearing a pretty noticeable amount of makeup. It wasn't the powder stuff like my mom normally wears though. It was the liquid stuff, but she'd done a horrible job at putting it on, because it was mostly packed around one eye. I asked her if she was trying out for the circus or if she was just covering up a black eye. She got all weird and ended our session on the spot."

Sheriff Laskey took down notes as to Shawn's claims, however, he remained doubtful due to the fact that Mrs. Schwartz had never reported the abuse to the police. "Did she ever actually admit to being abused?"

"She didn't have to. Everyone at school knew. It was common knowledge."

"Do you know of anyone who wasn't particularly fond of

Mrs. Schwartz?"

"Well, I wasn't too fond of her, but that doesn't mean you go around killing everyone you're not fond of."

Sheriff Laskey felt he'd gotten all the information he needed from him at that point, furthermore, he had other interviews to conduct that day. He certainly didn't have time to waste, swapping rebuttals with Shawn. "Okay, thank you for your time, Shawn. You can go now."

Relieved the questioning was over, Shawn got up with no hesitation and exited the room. The detective closed the door behind him. "So what do you think, Sheriff?"

"He's definitely hiding something. I just don't know if it pertains to Mrs. Schwartz. Let's follow up on the husband, for sure though. Meanwhile, go ahead and have the secretary call in the next kid on the list."

It wasn't long at all, before Detective O'Connell had returned with the next student, "Step inside and have a seat please," he instructed as he held the door open for Emma.

"Right here will be just fine," with a gesture of the hand Sheriff Laskey directed Emma to the seat opposite his. "Emma, I presume."

"Yes," Emma answered as she took her seat. She wasn't nervous, however, she wondered what they could possibly want to discuss with her.

Detective O'Connell took his place behind her and stood there, silently.

"I know you're wondering why we called you here. We just wanted to ask you a few routine questions, being that you were a patient of Mrs. Schwartz's. Maybe you can give us a little insight on the kind of person she was, and quite possibly, who she may have had dealings with."

"Well... I pretty much mind my own business, so I don't know how I could be of any assistance to you."

Sheriff Laskey looked down at his note pad. "It says here, you'd been seeing Mrs. Schwartz since your sophomore year here at Long Lake High School."

"Yeah. She was helping me to cope with some of the adversity I'm facing here at school."

"Adversity?" he questioned, tilting his head to the side.

"Mostly people bullying me for their own amusement. Mrs. Schwartz always stood up for me whenever she saw someone picking on me."

"She must have made some of the students angry in doing so?"

"They didn't really seem to care. You know teenagers... It's all a big joke to them."

"Do you know of anyone who wasn't particularly fond of Mrs. Schwartz?"

"No, not really. She was a truly compassionate woman. "I just..." Emma hesitated. Her eyes began to tear up. Still, she managed to control her emotions, knowing all too well what signs of weakness could lead to there at Long Lake. "I just really wished she had the confidence in herself that she had in others," Emma continued.

"So you feel she lacked confidence?"

"When it came to her personal life, yes."

"She's married though, right?" Of course, Sheriff Laskey already knew the answer. He was just fishing to see what Emma would say in response.

"That was the problem, if you ask me. Her husband was not a kind man. Some of the bruises she'd have when she came to school." Emma shook her head in despair. "You can just tell when someone is in a really bad situation. She never said anything, but I knew. So did everyone else."

"Emma, thank you for being so candid with me. You've been a tremendous help. I'm gonna let you go ahead and return to class now." Sheriff Laskey handed her a card with his name and number on it. "If you need anything, you can always contact me. I'm no Mrs. Schwartz by far, but I'm here to help if need be."

"Thanks." As Emma headed out of the room she contemplated telling them about the incident she'd encountered the previous night, but decided against it, figuring it was just more despicable behavior courtesy of a fellow student.

That night the streets were empty, with the exception of the patrolling officers. At last, the towns people were adhering to the curfew that had been set forth.

John sat on the couch in his apartment, combing through a scrapbook full of newspaper clippings detailing the string of murders that had been committed in Crimson County. He turned the page to an article covering the murder of Jennifer Nocks. The article displayed a photo of Jennifer, and beneath it the headline read: ANOTHER LOCAL TEEN SLAIN.

He flipped the next page in his scrapbook. It was blank. John rubbed a glue stick across the blank page for another clipping he'd planned to affix. He grabbed a newspaper article covering Shannon Rassner's murder from the pile of clippings beside him, then pressed it down onto the blank page. The article contained a photo of Shannon, and the headline read: CRIMSON COUNTY KILLER STRIKES AGAIN.

"Shannon Rassner," John whispered to himself, trying to recollect where he'd heard that name before.

Transfixed on Shannon's image, John soon became lost in thought. His memory took him back to a time when Samantha had not yet been taken from him. He was waiting outside of Long Lake High School when the final bell rang, signaling the end of the school day. The students began to trickle out of the school doors when Samantha and Shawn exited, walking directly toward John's truck. That particular day, Sam didn't look happy to see him, which was unusual. Her eyes were bloodshot and puffy. Her nose was beet red. Those few things made it quite evident to him that she'd been crying. The two climbed into the vehicle, Sam in front and Shawn in the back seat. Sam sat facing straight ahead with her head bowed, so her long brown hair draped over the sides of her face. John lifted his hand, brushing her hair back behind her left ear. "Sam, what's wrong?" He waited a few seconds for an answer that didn't come. John turned to Shawn for some insight on the situation. "Shawn, what's wrong with your sister?"

"I don't know, Dad. She won't tell me either?"

Sam sniffled, just before letting out a heavy sigh, then with a gentle voice said, "Everything's okay, Dad."

"It sure doesn't appear that way, Sam."

"Just another day at Long Lake High, starring Shannon Rassner and the lovely Jennifer Nocks, featuring us."

"Well, sweetie what did they do to upset you like this?"

"It's nothing, Dad. Just leave it alone."

Much to his dismay, he complied not wanting to press the issue any further for fear of upsetting her even more than she already was. John shifted the truck into drive, and in that instant the memory faded, bringing him back to reality. John leaned back on the couch, closing the scrap book.

10

That afternoon, Sheriff Laskey sat at his desk reviewing case files, when Detective O'Connell entered his office. "I talked to Mrs. Schwartz's estranged husband."

Sheriff Laskey paused, glancing up at him, "And," he replied, eagerly awaiting what it was the detective had come to tell him.

"He's on his way in for questioning. Actually, he should be here any minute."

"He's coming to us? That's a first."

"Well, it turns out he and Linda are still married, just as we suspected. Technically, they were just separated, never really finalizing the divorced. So, he's really coming under the assumption that he's retrieving her belongings that we've confiscated."

"The case is still open. He can't retrieve anything yet. That's evidence."

"Of course. I know that, but he doesn't." Detective O'Connell paused, lifting an eyebrow. "Catch my drift?"

"Ahhh," Sheriff Laskey replied, finally realizing what Detective O'Connell had done. "Way to get the suspect in, Detective... I couldn't have handled it better myself."

About thirty minutes had past, by the time a rugged forty-something, Mr. Schwartz, entered the police station. He was dressed in jeans, a flannel shirt and a blue jean jacket.

Tape covered the bridge of his obviously broken nose. He headed straight for the front counter, where a female officer was stationed.

"Eh em," Mr. Schwartz cleared his throat in an effort at gaining the attention of the female officer, who was preoccupied reading a report. The officer quickly raised her head. "Oh," she said, initially put off by the broken nose and bruising around his eyes.

"Yeah... I'm here to see Detective O'Connell."

"And you are?"

Mr. Schwartz stiffened. Standing up straight, believing he'd shook off any nuances of weakness.

"Mr. Schwartz. My wife was murdered. I'm here to collect her belongings."

She was taken back by his callus demeanor. He said that with such ease, she thought.

"Wait here," she instructed, just before walking off to make Detective O'Connell aware of his arrival.

Meanwhile, an impatient, Mr. Schwartz paced the floor of the waiting area.

After letting him stew for a little more than fifteen minutes, Detective O'Connell strolled up to the counter, buzzing him through the waist high door. "Mr. Schwartz?"

"That's me."

"Come on back."

Mr. Schwartz huffed, "It's about time," he whispered, pushing through the door.

Detective O'Connell escorted him back to Sheriff Laskey's office for questioning, where the sheriff was still seated behind his desk.

"Have a seat, sir," Detective O'Connell instructed as they both entered Sheriff Laskey's office. Mr. Schwartz's eyebrows wrinkled. As he'd taken his seat he thought to himself, all this just to collect a few belongings.

"Thank you for coming in, Mr. Schwartz. I'm Sheriff Laskey. I just need to ask you a few routine questions."

"That's some damage there, by the way," Sheriff Laskey pointed out as he leaned back in his chair. "If you don't mind me asking, how did that happen?"

Mr. Schwartz glanced back at Detective O'Connell, who stood there with his arms folded. An attempt at intimidation, no doubt. Mr. Schwartz snickered at him, letting the detective know that his attempt at intimidation had failed miserably.

"I was in a bar fight," he sarcastically replied, while shooting him a condescending look. "I thought I was here to pick up my wife's belongings?"

"Well, as I just informed the detective, the case is still open. That means the items we confiscated will remain in our possession for the time being. Now, Mr. Schwartz do you know of anyone who'd have a reason to harm your wife?"

"No Sheriff, I don't."

Considering he wasn't accustomed to being spoken to in such a demanding tone, he did a good job at keeping his cool. After all, he couldn't knock around, nor emotionally abuse authorities, as he'd done his late wife.

"And where were you on Saturday night, between the hours of nine o'clock and twelve midnight?"

"I was at home."

Sheriff Laskey stared at him, as if by staring long enough, he could cause him to contradict his statement. Unfortunately for him, Mr. Schwartz didn't budge.

"Do you have anyone who can corroborate what you're telling us?"

Mr. Schwartz's demeanor went from calm to defensive in seconds. He leaned forward in his chair, "No. Wait, wait, wait... You think I killed my wife?!"

"Now, hold on... I didn't say that. We just have to cover all the bases," Sheriff Laskey assured him.

He didn't want to anger, or make him feel as if they thought he was guilty. Sheriff Laskey needed to get as much information out of him as possible, before he would inevitably decide to lawyer up. Mr. Schwartz leaned back in his chair. The sheriff's rebuttal was enough to defuse his defenses for the time being.

"How was your relationship with your wife?"

In that moment, Mr. Schwartz had imagined himself blurting out, "I beat the shit out of her, whenever the little bitch got out of line. Any other questions?" causing the officers jaws to drop in disbelief as he beamed, swollen with pride.

However in reality, because he was a man who wished to remain free from imprisonment, he uttered a less gratifying response instead. "Like every relationship, we had our ups and downs."

Sheriff Laskey felt cheated by his response and was eager to get the truth, once and for all. "Did you beat your wife, Mr. Schwartz?"

Mr. Schwartz hopped up from his chair. They'd entered a territory he cared not to peruse. "What kind of question is that?"

Convinced that rumors were true, he angered, hardening his tone. "A very simple one. Did you beat your wife?" Sheriff Laskey had to be direct with his questioning. There was no way around it, if he expected to get the answers he was looking for.

"I think my lawyer should be present for these questions."

"Do you have something to hide?"

At that point, he'd made up his mind. Mr. Schwartz was through with being questioned. Sheriff Laskey had pressed too far too soon.

"Are you arresting me?"

"Not at the moment."

"Then, I'm leaving."

What a spineless piece of shit, Sheriff Laskey thought. Yet, there wasn't a thing he could do to stop him from walking out of that office, and back into the community.

Sheriff Laskey was fuming. He thought it best not to comment any further, so he shrugged his shoulders, before glancing over at Detective O'Connell.

The detective pushed aside his feelings of reluctance, then opened the door to allow Mr. Schwartz to walk out, but couldn't resist the urge to slam the door behind him.

"Quite the loathsome individual," Detective O'Connell remarked in a quieted voice.

Mr. Schwartz tore angrily through the police station, smashing into Shawn, who happened to be on his way back to find Sheriff Laskey.

Shawn stopped abruptly, "Hey buddy, I'm walking here."

Mr. Schwartz turned, fixing his eyes on him, at which point Shawn realized Mr. Schwartz may be more trouble than it's worth, so he decided to let it go. "My fault, dude. Looks like you've had a bad day," Shawn said throwing up his hands, before continuing on his way.

Detective O'Connell had come out of the sheriff's office, just as Shawn approached. "Shawn, what are you doing here?"

"I was wondering if I could get that tape?"

His eyebrows raised, now even more suspicious of Shawn's motives. "The case is still open. We have to keep all evidence sealed until otherwise, son. You signed the release."

"I just don't want my parents to hear it."

"Well... since you didn't release it to your parents, they have no right to hear what's on the tape."

Shawn let out a sigh of relief. "Okay."

"I think you should head home, before it gets dark."

"Yeah, I guess you're right."

Shawn headed out of the building, being studied by the detective until he exited the doors.

Later that night, Detective O'Connell stormed into Sheriff Laskey's office eager to report his latest findings. "Sheriff, you won't believe this."

"Try me," the sheriff requested, yet at the same time thought, this better be good news because I don't think the situation could get any worse.

"I pulled Mr. Schwartz's record. Turns out he's been arrested multiple times for aggravated assault. Mrs. Schwartz had also filed a domestic violence suit against him. They were scheduled to go to trial next month. And here's the kicker. Jennifer Nocks and Shannon Rassner were testifying against him. It seems, they witnessed him assaulting Mrs. Schwartz on several occasions."

"Well, I'll be damned... A reason to kill," Sheriff Laskey proclaimed as he leaned forward in his office chair, pointing his forefinger at Detective O'Connell. "Ya see, it always comes back to motive. Most anybody can be compelled to murder. The key is finding out the reason why your specific victim was chosen. That's all the answer you need. Motive... Now we've got the son of a bitch by the wrinkly sacs."

Sheriff Laskey stood abruptly. "Damn it, O'Connell! We just had the bastard here. Why are we just now finding out about this?!"

"Well... he lives in Santa Fair County, which happens to be where the incidents took place. Therefore, the complaint was filed with their precinct."

"I think we've found our killer. I'll call Judge Walker. We need an arrest warrant, tonight. Sheriff Laskey sprung into action. He snatched up the phone receiver to dial Judge Walker, post haste.

Meanwhile, Mr. Schwartz had made it home. He stormed into the house, yanking off his jacket, then flung it onto the floor as he paced angrily across the foyer. It took a moment for him to calm, but he was successful after having contemplated his next move. He picked up his coat, hung it on the coat rack near the front door, then grabbed his cell phone from his pants pocket, with intentions to phone his lawyer.

No more than an hour later, Detective O'Connell along with a female officer were knocking at his front door, while additional officers surrounded the house.

Mr. Schwartz had already batten down for the night, so when he exited his bedroom to answer the door, he was only wearing his boxers briefs and a t-shirt. "Just a minute. This better be good," he mumbled, making his way toward the front door.

"Who is it?" he grumbled, impatiently waiting for a response.

"It's the police, Mr. Schwartz. Open up!" Detective O'Connell shouted through the front door.

Mr. Schwartz hesitated initially, but soon came to the conclusion that he had no other choice, so he begrudgingly granted the detective's request. Detective O'Connell stood there with a smirk on his face as he held up the warrant. He was all too happy to have served him.

"Mr. Schwartz you're under arrest for the murder of your wife, Linda Schwartz. Turn around and put your hands behind your back."

Mr. Schwartz was shocked, almost in complete disbelief of what was taking place. Detective O'Connell grabbed his arm, spun him around, then slapped the cuffs on his wrists, before the realization of the situation finally set in, compelling him to speak. "I want to call my lawyer."

"Of course you do. That can wait until we get to the station," Detective O'Connell said as he escorted him outside. "You have the right to remain silent. Anything you say can and will be used against you in a court of law. You have the right to an attorney. If you can not afford an attorney, one will be appointed to you. Do you understand these rights, as I have explained them to you?"

"Can I at least get a pair of pants on?"

"One of the officers will get a pair for you. Just keep it moving to the squad car, buddy."

Two other officers walked past Mr. Schwartz and Detective O'Connell as they were headed inside the home.

One officer went straight to Mr. Schwartz's bedroom to begin his search for evidence. He lifted the mattress, allowing the pillows to slide off onto the floor. Nothing was there. He moved to the dresser, where he'd begun to riffle through the drawers, while a second officer had already started his search of the living room.

The second officer tossed the couch cushions onto the floor, then slid his gloved hands into the cracks of the sofa.

Meanwhile, the female officer caught a glimpse of something on the foyer floor, where Mr. Schwartz had previously thrown his jacket. She put on her latex gloves, before she walked over, picking it up. It was a gold necklace with a crucifix pendant. "This sure doesn't look like a necklace that a man would wear," the officer mumbled quietly, to herself.

Having gotten Mr. Schwartz secure in the squad car, Detective O'Connell entered the home wearing latex gloves, eager to join the search and seizure. "Did you find something?"

"A necklace," she answered as she held it up for him to see.

Detective O'Connell tilted his head. Seeing the necklace had triggered something in his mind. "I've seen that somewhere before. Wait a minute," he paused, searching his memory for a brief moment. Sure enough, he was able to recollect where he thought he'd seen it. "Do you still have the picture Mrs. Nocks gave us of Jennifer?"

"It's in the glove compartment. I'll go get it."

The officer handed the necklace over to Detective O'Connell, "Here, you take this," she instructed, before heading out the door.

"Actually, you know what? I'm right behind you," he said, hastily tagging along. Detective O'Connell was positive he'd seen the necklace before, and couldn't bare waiting until the female officer returned with the photo, just to find out if his memory had served him correctly.

She opened the car door, then retrieved the photograph out of an envelope in the glove compartment. "Oh my God, you were right," she declared, only having glanced at the image for a second, before handing it over to the detective.

The moment O'Connell laid eyes on the photo, he saw the necklace as plain as day, hanging around Jennifer's neck. His heart sank. She'd worn that necklace when she was alive and well, only now it was in their possession, having been snatched off of her lifeless body. He'd seen her battered flesh. He'd smelled her rotting corpse. He'd endured looking into Mrs. Nocks' eyes, while having to inform her that her daughter had been murdered just beyond the safety of their home. It was almost too much for him to handle. "I knew I'd seen it before," he sadly admitted, before handing the necklace over to the female officer, "Bag that for prints."

11

The following day, Steven entered a room in the morgue, locking the door behind him. He looked much different than the Steven that Megan, John and Linda had previously made acquaintance with. He was wearing a white lab coat over his clothing. As opposed to being gelled back, his hair was parted down the middle, free to hang just over his ear lobes. His eyes were brown instead of the usual blue, but he was wearing eyeglasses, therefore he didn't need his contact lenses. There was also a small white bandage on his forehead, covering a cut just above his right eye.

He stood with his back to the door, scanning the room with his eyes. Most of the corpses were stored in the compartment trays along the wall, with the exception of one. It was exactly what he was looking for. Steven moved over to a stainless steel table where the single corpse laid covered, then proceeded to pull the sheet down below the corpse's abdomen. Linda Schwartz, laid there cold and pale. Her lips had taken an ashen color, being that most of the blood had drained from her body.

Steven rubbed his fingertips between her breasts, traveling down the middle of her torso, then along her belly button. To him, her cold skin felt as smooth as silk. He pressed his ear to her chest, as if he were listening for a heartbeat. "Nope," he whispered devilishly.

The smell of formaldehyde, which exuded from the pores of her skin seemed to further comfort him as he took in a whiff, savoring her essence. Steven lifted his head just enough to give the corpse a peck on the lips, while caressing her stiffened breast with his left hand. Innately aroused, he unzipped his pants with his right, allowing his bulging member to poke through the opening. As Steven had begun to masturbate, he kissed her upon the lips once more, only this time with added aggression. He mashed his lips against hers, then down along her neckline, breathing like a charging bull. Steven's heart beat began to thump as he was overcome with excitement. He jerked faster and faster. He panted harder and harder. Finally he ejaculated, resting his head upon her chest. Once his breathing had regulated, he straightened his fogged glasses, then wiped the semen from his hand onto the sheet that covered her corpse. Steven zipped his pants, feeling not only satisfied, but more importantly reborn.

Across town, Shawn rested on his bed. With his hands folded behind his head, he stared up at the ceiling, listening to music on his iPod. He'd stayed home from school that day, claiming to be plagued by migraines.

A few knocks on his bedroom door went unanswered, before Megan called out to him. "Shawn! Shawn!" Still he couldn't hear her. But, between being dismissed by John and being mislead by Ron, she was at her wits end. There was no doubt in her mind that he was in the room. So refusing to be ignored, Megan pushed open the door. "Shawn!"

Catching him off guard the way she had, caused him to hop up, instantly snatching the earphones out of his ears. "Geez... I guess we don't knock anymore," he spouted angrily.

"I did knock. So I guess that would mean, you just don't listen anymore," Megan snapped back without hesitation.

He looked at her with a blank stare. However, not too eager to match wits with her at that moment, Shawn plopped back down on the mattress. "What do you want, Mom?"

"I just wanted to talk," she passively replied as she walked over, taking a seat on the edge of his bed.

Here we go, he thought, bracing himself. "What could we possibly have to talk about?"

"Shawn, I know you've been going through a lot lately. Losing Samantha was hard on all of us. I just wanted to find out how you've been handling all this. I'm sure that with all that's been going on lately, it's brought back memories of Samantha's death."

Shawn leaned back on the headboard, somewhat defused by her inquiry. "I don't want to talk about that."

"I'm trying my best to reach out to you, Shawn. You've got to meet me halfway."

"I said, I don't want to talk about it," Shawn reasserted as he turned his back to her, putting in his earphones.

Megan let out a long sigh of frustration, but she was determined not to let Shawn's sour attitude ruin the evening she had planned with Steven.

"I understand." As opposed to pushing the issue, she

headed for her room to get ready for her date.

After she'd finally gotten dressed, she stood there and stared at herself in the large mirror that sat atop her dresser. Megan shrugged her shoulders, feeling her appearance could be improved upon. So she opened the makeup bag on the dresser, then went to work on her profile.

Shawn stood watching from the doorway, with a most unpleasant look upon his face. He wasn't too happy about her getting all dolled up for someone other than his father. He wondered what she was thinking as she covered her face in pressed powder. He thought to himself, why did she stop doing these things for my dad, as she applied her eyeshadow. Shawn attempted to search his mind for a justifiable reason for the deceitful things she'd done in the past, as she brushed rouge blush about her cheekbones.

All the while, she hadn't noticed him there. "Mom," he called out to her, finally gaining her attention.

"You going somewhere?"

"I'm meeting someone for a late lunch," she answered, casually applying her makeup.

Shawn seethed with resentment, "Tell Ron I hope he chokes on his fries."

"Oh Shawn... stop it. I'm not even going with Ron."

Being that his interest was peaked, Shawn moved closer toward her. Maybe she was meeting his dad, he'd hoped. "Oh yeah, then who are you going with?"

"His name is Steven. He seems like a nice guy. I bumped into him yesterday, when I was picking up some clothes from the dry cleaners," she explained delightfully, as if she'd done a good job by opting for someone other than Ron.

His feelings of disapproval resurfaced with the wrinkling of his eyebrows. His shoulders slumped as he shook his head in utter disappointment. "There's a murderer on the loose, and you're going out to lunch with some random guy?! Why am I even surprised? Classic, Mom..."

She could see his blank stare through the reflection in the mirror. It bothered her so much so, that a corner of her mouth began to twitch from embarrassment. She was so consumed with jealousy over Ron's public displays of affection with another woman, that the murders hadn't even crossed her mind at the time. She had already been wrong in various other situations, Megan couldn't bear to admit that he was right about this.

"That's how you get to know people, Shawn," she responded, rapidly stroking her eyebrows with the brush that applied her black mascara.

"Whatever," he whispered. With his hopes now crushed, he turned to walk out of her room, but couldn't bring himself to leave without getting out one last comment. "You know what, Mom... There's so much about you I just don't get." Shawn stormed out, slamming the door behind him.

Megan's hands dropped onto her lap, she closed her eyes, then took a deep breath, attempting to maintain her composure. Shawn had bothered her conscience, yet unfortunately not enough to stop her from being the kind of woman she truly was.

Back at the morgue Steven had set up shop in the men's restroom to get ready for his evening with Megan. A black gym bag sat open on the sink. He had packed it with everything he would need for his transformation.

First Steven removed his glasses, but swapped them with blue contact lenses. Next, he removed his lab coat and white button up shirt, which were replaced with a black, fitted, v-neck t-shirt. He then applied a generous amount of gel to his hair, so that it slicked it back nice and neat. Finally, he snatched off the bandage on his forehead. Steven stared into the mirror, flexing his chest with confidence. In his mind he was his alter ego, a completely different person.

Meanwhile, Megan was ready. She trotted out the front door in her heels and short black dress over to her old, yet surprisingly clean, 4X4 jeep, parked in the driveway. She got in, and whipped her long black hair behind her shoulder, then turned the key in the ignition. Even though the engine didn't start, Megan refrained from panic. This wasn't out of the ordinary. Sometimes it just needed a little help. Megan tried again, only this time she pumped her foot down on the gas pedal, "Come on, baby," she said encouragingly as she turned the key a second time. The exhaust choked and the car puttered. Finally it started, but ultimately failed again, before she could shift the gear into drive.

"Come on. Come on. Damn it!"

She took her cell phone out of her small black handbag, dialing Steven, who just so happened to answer on the first ring. "Well, hello," he answered, as if he'd already been expecting her call.

She was flattered by him answering the phone so quickly. "Wow. That was fast. Uh, I've got a slight problem, though."

"You're not canceling on me are you?" he asked confidently.

"Of course not, but my car won't start. I was wondering if you could pick me up, if it's not too much trouble?"

"Sure, no problem."

"Okay. Great."

"See ya soon."

Megan tilted her head to one side. He doesn't even have the address, she thought. "Wait, don't you need my address?"

"Oh yeah, the address," he replied, pretending not to know.

"It's 1016 Cozen Drive."

"I'm not too far from there."

"Okay, I'll wait outside for you then."

Megan was determined not to go back inside of the house, for fear that Shawn would be even more upset that she planned to ride with Steven, instead of meeting him for their date.

About ten minutes had past by the time Steven pulled up in front of her house, in his black, vintage, t-top Camero. Having anticipated his arrival, Megan stepped daintily off the porch and strutted down the walkway toward him. He watched her as she approached, then leaned in through the passenger side window, taking the opportunity to flash him a little cleavage.

"I guess you didn't have any trouble finding the house."

He wasn't impressed by her slutty gesture. What a desperate and lazy attempt at gaining a man's attention, he thought. But, of course he wasn't about to tell Megan how he truly felt.

"I know these streets like the back of my hand. Hop in."

"I like your car," she remarked, conceding his request.

"Of course you do," he mumbled, before commenting aloud. "Thanks. I try to take good care of her."

Megan smiled, charmed by his reply, being that she'd neglected to hear his initial comment. She'd made an assumption, equating that because he referred to his vehicle, of which he takes such great care, as "her," that possibly he'd treat her with the same benevolence.

"Her?" She questioned, fishing for more clues that would reveal a bit more about his character.

Steven knew exactly what she was up to, and was certainly

not going to oblige her. "It's a guy thing."

"I bet."

Megan's eyes studied his face. It wasn't long before the miniscule scratch on his forehead caught her attention. "So, what happened there?" She gestured her pointer finger toward his right eyebrow, "Was that a guy thing, too?"

"This," he responded, rubbing his finger across the injury. "Oh, hazards of work... It's nothing."

Steven started his car, then revved the engine in an attempt to steer her focus from his facial blemish, before he pulling off.

"So, exactly what is it you do for a living?"

"I don't know if I should tell you. I wouldn't want to freak you out on our first date."

"You'd be surprised at how much it would take to freak me out."

He was reluctant to reveal his occupation, but simply blurted it out, getting it over with quickly, so they could move past it. "I work at the county morgue. I am, by all accounts, a mortician."

Just as he'd predicted, she was a bit taken back by his line of work, however someone's got to do it, she thought. "The morgue." Megan paused, in contemplation of the recent string of fatalities around town. Her tone softened, "I guess you've been awfully busy then."

"To say the least," he replied, softening his tone as well.

Back at the sheriff's department, Sheriff Laskey made his way through the station, coffee in hand. A female officer was seated at a desk just outside of his office.

"Mr. Slater is waiting for you in your office," she warned, stopping him in his tracks.

His agitation had immediately begun to brew, while nervousness simmered in his belly. He had no concrete answers for John, as to the identity of Samantha's killer. Nor was he in the frame of mind to listen to one of John's angry tirades about the police department's lack of urgency in finding the perpetrator.

"Why?"

She was well aware of the reason for John's visit, however, she wanted nothing to do with the situation, let alone to discuss it while John waited just within ear shot of their conversation. In a more quieted voice, she answered, "Your guess is as good as mine."

"Just what I need," Sheriff Laskey mumbled, begrudgingly opening his office door.

"Mr. Slater," he greeted him upon entering his office, to the site of John pacing the floor. "Is there a problem?"

John paused, "I heard you have a suspect in custody."

The sheriff sipped his coffee, searching his mind for a fitting response. "A suspect," he replied, in a matter of fact tone, before he took a seat in his chair, "That would be accurate."

John sat as well, responding without hesitation. "Did he kill my daughter?"

"Well... now, hold on. We can't be sure of that just yet. He won't talk without his attorney present. Besides, he can only be linked to three of the most recent murders. Not your daughter's."

John angered instantly, hopping back up from his chair. "What about the others?"

"We have no motive, let alone evidence to connect them," the sheriff answered.

"Motive! Damn it, let me talk to him! I'll get your motive! I mean... Come on, Sheriff." Every word John uttered seemed to be accompanied by droplets of saliva. His face had turned beet red as the veins bulged from his neck.

Sheriff Laskey sat the coffee mug down on his desk, gesturing at John to lower his voice. "I'm sorry, as much as I'd like to, I can't let you do that. You have to let us handle this, John. The last thing we need is him getting off on grounds of battery or harassment. Trust me. If this is our guy, he's going to pay for what he's done."

Over at Ron's house, he and his date from the bistro, had just burst through his bedroom door in the throws of a passionate embrace. Ron snatched open her shirt, unlatching the metal clasps all in a single motion. He rubbed his hands over her breast, back, and shoulders. She took deep breaths in anticipation of his every move.

Pressed against one another in a frenzy of heat and lust, they kissed as the last of their clothing came off in seconds. A playfully shove sent him falling back onto the bed as she danced erotically, waving her hips around as a teaser. When she climbed on top of him, her long blonde hair draped down over his face as she ground her pelvis against his. Ron rolled her onto her back, then lifted his body over top of hers. Her legs opened with ease as he grabbed her hip with one hand to thrust deep inside her. Ron began to thrust harder, then faster. With every deep stroke her eyes seemed to roll back deeper into their lids. Her back stiffened in an arch as she could only concentrate on the feeling of him inside her. Her hands gripped his back as she yelled out in ecstasy. Finally, he grunted. They'd climaxed in unison.

Ron rolled over on his back. They panted, with smiles planted firmly about their faces. He reached over, grabbing a lighter and cigarette off of the nightstand, then proceeded to smoke. She felt satisfied with the catch she'd made. As she snuggled up close to him, with the palm of her hand resting upon his chest, she felt his heart racing. "You're sweating, too. It must have been as good for you as it was for me."

Ron's mood changed instantly. His mouth twisted into a mirthless smile, it was there and gone in a flash. "I doubt it," he countered, in the driest of tones.

"What?" She couldn't believe her ears. What happened? Did I say something wrong, she thought.

Ron felt compelled to clarify his blatant response, that way she'd get the point sooner than later. "I've had better."

Taken aback, she moved away from him, but at the same time, pulled the sheet up to her chest to cover her dangling breast. She hadn't known him but a couple of days, and already she was embarrassed that she'd given in to his advances, so easily. "What an asshole you turned out to be."

"Tell me something I don't know."

Her jaw dropped. The woman scoffed, appalled by the way he was treating her. She flung the sheet angrily as she hopped out of bed to get dressed. Her voice cracked, "Take me home, now," she demanded as she buttoned her capri pants.

Ron grabbed his jeans from the edge of the bed, took a fifty dollar bill from the front pocket, then tossed the money at her dismissively, as if she were a prostitute, and their business there had been concluded. "Call a cab."

The woman quickly bent over to snatch up the fifty dollar bill, "Fuck you, you prick." But instead of balling it up and throwing it in his face, like her first mind had instructed, she slid it into her pocket, having remembered she had no alternative means of making it home.

"No thanks. I don't want seconds. And good grief, hurry up and put on your shirt. Your saggy tits are making me nauseous."

The small of her back stiffened, she lifted her shoulders, standing up tall, but avoided making eye contact with Ron.

At that point, the self consciousness he'd caused her to feel had become noticeable, even as she knelt to pick up her shirt. Her hands quivered as she snapped each button. Trying to maintain what little dignity she had left, she mashed her lips together, in an attempt to stop her top lip from twitching. The sting she felt in her nostrils had caused her eyes to water. Still, Ron could see that tears were imminent.

How could he be so deliberately hurtful, she thought? There was nothing she could say to help him understand how ugly he'd made her feel, although it was apparent Ron wouldn't care either way. She realized what a horrible mistake she'd made by sleeping with him, so she remained silent, even as the tears streamed down her cheeks.

At the same time that Ron was doing his best to rip his date's confidence to shreds, on the other side of town, Shawn and Emma laid in his bed nestled close to one another.

Her head rested upon his chest, while he ran his fingers across her long, curly locks. He was always different with her than others, but she'd noticed a slight change in his behavior. There were so many things that could have caused the shift in his demeanor, she thought. Maybe it was the fact that the anniversary of Samantha's death had just passed. Maybe it was the finalization of his parents' divorce. Could it be the murders? Either way she was determined to help Shawn through it.

"What's wrong, Shawn? You've been acting different lately."

"Nothing's wrong, Emma."

"You know you can tell me anything. I'm here no matter what... Even if it's just to talk."

He rubbed his finger tips down her stomach, then along her navel. "Anything?" he asked, hinting it be sexual in nature.

She stopped him, gently grabbing his hand, "Shawn, I'm serious."

"I know you are, but I'll be fine. I've just got a lot on my mind. It'll pass. I promise." Shawn kissed her atop her head.

"I wish everything wasn't so screwed up." Emma paused. "And at school... don't get me started. I hate having to hide our relationship," she continued.

"We don't have to hide anything," Shawn assured her.

"Everybody thinks I'm a loser, and if they find out I've got the most handsome guy at school, they'll really be out for blood. No thanks... I've got enough on my plate."

"What do you mean, don't get you started? Is something else going on, I don't know about?"

Emma sat up, then took a deep breath. "Okay," she exhaled. "I've gotta to tell you something... But, you have to promise me you're not gonna get all upset."

Emma didn't want Shawn to overact and do something foolish, but at the same time she didn't want to keep any secrets from him.

Shawn nudged her cheek, turning her eyes on him. "What is it?"

"The night of the candlelight vigil... I was kind of attacked."

"What?!" Shawn sat up on the bed, shocked and quite frankly infuriated by her admission. He wasn't sure what to think. "What do you mean, kind of attacked? Who attacked you?"

"I'm not sure. The guy was wearing a ski mask. He grabbed me in the parking lot."

Shawn jumped out of bed. "What the hell, Emma?! Why are you just now saying something? Did you call the cops? What happened?"

"Shawn, just calm down. I'm okay. And no, I didn't call the police. It could have just as easily been a student pulling a prank on me. I'm not exactly part of the in crowd."

He paced the floor in conflict of what he should do about the situation.

"What the fuck?! Who does that?!"

There were so many thoughts running through his mind. What if it had been a fellow student? They'd gone too far this time. This had to stop. He also considered the fact that it could have been an attempt to take her life? I should have been there to protect her, he blamed himself. I can't bear losing Emma, too.

She saw the torment he was taking himself through, and in that moment she'd regretted telling him. He'd already been through so much in regards to his family's misfortune.

"If it makes you feel any better, I gave him a pretty good beating."

"Did you?" He paused, somewhat pacified by the thought of her finally standing up for herself.

Emma hopped out of bed, sporting a smile, "Of course I did."

"Hi yah," she said as she chopped her hand down playfully, demonstrating a martial arts defensive technique.

Shawn grinned, letting out a slight chuckle, "Okay... hi yah..."

"Come here." He wrapped one arm around Emma's waist, then pulled her toward him, into a tender kiss.

In the mist of their passionate lip lock, Shawn inched her backward toward the bed.

Emma had reluctantly put on the brakes, pressing her hands gently upon his chest. "I have to get home, before it gets too late. It's gonna be dark soon, and I wouldn't wanna have to kick somebody's ass again."

Shawn exhaled, temporarily forcing back his sexual urges. "Whoa... you're an ass kicker now? Somebody's gaining confidence. Well, I'll walk you home anyway. That should actually buy us some time. About five minutes, maybe," he said, with hopes that she'd stay.

He moved in once more, then slowly kissed her lips. "Maybe, ten," Shawn reasoned, as he brushed her curls behind her back to kiss her upon the tip of her exposed shoulder. Emma nibbled her bottom lip, relishing the moment. "Fifteen," he whispered, before kissing her a third time upon the neck. Shawn tasted her ear lobe with the tip of his tongue. Emma's heart raced. She winced from the tingling she felt in her core, just before he playfully pushed her back onto the bed. She could no longer resist. Emma wanted him just as much as he did her. "I think it'll still be daylight by then," Emma agreed as she tugged at his t-shirt to pull him down on top of her."

Meanwhile back at John's apartment, he sat on the couch, contemplating his next move. How was Mr. Schwartz linked to his daughter, he thought? There had to be something he'd overlooked, something that could help him find the motive they needed. More importantly, the motive he needed to exact his revenge.

He walked over to the closet, taking down a large shoe box labeled SAM, from the top shelf. John took it back over to the sofa to skim through it for clues. He'd never gone through the box in its entirety. Every time he'd make an attempt to, combing through her pictures proved too difficult for his heart to take. This time he had to be strong for the sake of proving Mr. Schwartz was indeed the monster that had taken Sam's life, ruined his family, and terrorized their small town.

First, he grabbed a small pillow from the box with her name embroidered on the front. He flipped it over to reveal the words, *daddy's little girl,* stitched on the back. John closed his eyes as he ran his finger tips along the threaded lettering, simmering in the emotions brought about by memories of him presenting the pillow to his precious daughter. Sam was just seven years old at the time. The pillow was meant to comfort her on nights he'd worked late and wasn't able to make it home soon enough to tuck her into bed. Memories that would have normally brought him to tears, had then given John the extra push he needed to continue searching through her belongings. Fighting the impulse to fall apart, John took a deep breath, before opening his eyes, determined to find what he was looking for.

He pulled out a hand sized light weight metal lock box that had been stuffed under some of Sam's old birthday cards. He hadn't noticed it being stashed there before, nor did he remember ever seeing it while Sam was still living. John attempted to lift the lid. He pressed his thumb down on a small metal lever that should have released the hinge, allowing the box to open. But, it was locked. He leaned back on the sofa, pulling a Swiss Army Knife from the front pocket of his jeans. Using it to pry open the lock, he'd busted it in the process.

John lifted the lid to find it was filled with photos, letters, and small notes that were hand written on loose leaf paper. He unfolded one of the old wrinkled notes. It read, *will you go out with me, check yes or no.* John smirked, it had to have been written by a young boy who had a crush on her long ago, he thought. He dug under the letters, grabbing a stack of photos that she'd rubber banded together. The first of the pictures was of Sam and a young boy with whom she'd attended grade school. Of course he was curious to see the others, so he unraveled them, moving on to the next photo.

The next one was also a picture of Sam. An image of her kissing someone whose face wasn't visible, due to the fact that the photo was taken from a side angle. As John came upon the third photo, he lifted his hand, covering his mouth in disbelief. Sam was dressed in a short red teddy, posed with her arms and legs sprawled out across her bed. She'd gazed directly into the camera with the intent of being enticing. He was shocked that his little girl would take a picture so sexual in nature. Like most fathers, he thought his daughter had maintained her fidelity. Still, he loved Sam and valued her innocence. There had to be something that pushed her to do this, he told himself as he flipped to the next photo to find out exactly what that something could be.

John's heart dropped to his stomach. Devastation overwhelmed him as he fixed his eyes on a picture of Sam and Ron lying in the nude. Ron slept as Sam rested her head upon his hairy chest. One of her arms were stretched out, holding the camera in order to capture the explicit moment without Ron's knowledge. Not only had John's ex-best friend helped himself to his wife, but he'd also deflowered his daughter. How could John have been so blind and clueless as to what was going on right under his nose? His body trembled as the anger boiled up inside of him. Overtaken by his impulses, John ripped the picture into small pieces. "Son of a bitch! Not my daughter!"

He slammed his fists down on the coffee table in a rage, causing the glass to shatter into what seemed like a million pieces, which scattered across the hardwood floor. John bolted out of the apartment, leaving his front door wide open. Ron had crossed him for the last time. He hopped in his truck, headed straight for Ron's house, only five minutes away.

Dusk approached. The streets were clear. It seemed as if the town had been abandoned, for most were locked safely in their homes. John sped down the streets of Crimson, tires screeching, burning rubber, with complete disregard of all traffic lights and stop signs. Having shortened his driving time to just a few minutes, John slammed on his brakes in front of Ron's house and jumped out of the truck, leaving it running.

He leaped up the porch, two stairs at a time, then slammed his fist against the front door. BANG! BANG! BANG! BANG! BANG!

Ron jumped up from the bed, grabbing his robe. "What the fuck?! Did you call a cab or the cops??"

The woman stayed put at the edge of the bed, smoking a cigarette as Ron headed out of the room for the front door. "Well, come on. Get your shit together. Your cab's here."

She shook her head in utter disappointment. Between her smeared red lipstick and the black mascara that had run down her cheeks accompanied by her tears, her face was a cosmetic disaster.

John paced the porch, peering in through the windows to

see if Ron was home. "RON! RON!"

"I'm coming! I'm coming!" he yelled, yet at the same time wondered how the cab driver knew his name.

Ron peeked through the peephole, "Who is it?"

Just when he'd put his eye up to the door, John lifted his right leg high, thrusting the bottom of his boot into the door. The front door went flying open, cracking Ron in the forehead. The blow sent him staggering back, stunned and dazed. John spared him no expense, tackling him back onto the side table along the wall. Golf trophies, picture frames, and a vase all dropped to the floor along with Ron's limp body. John stomped down on his rib cage with as much force as he could muster. He groaned, curled up in the fetal position with his arms wrapped, covering his abdomen. "What the fuck, man?" He wasn't sure yet why John was attacking him. They'd come to terms long ago, as far as he and Megan's affair.

"You, motherfucker!" John dropped to his knees, getting a tight grip on the collar of Ron's robe. "My daughter, huh?! My daughter!"

Ron's eyes grew wide. He was frozen in fear. Then he knew.

With closed fist, John rained down blows to Ron's face again and again, pummeling him within an inch of his life. By the time John felt compelled to stop, his hands were covered in blood, and Ron's face was barely recognizable. The blood oozed down his face. Not only had his lips and nose already begun to swell, one of his eyes were also swollen shut. He coughed, gasping for air, almost choking on the blood that had flooded his throat from the gaping wounds in his mouth.

John was nearly out of breath, when he lifted to his feet. Beads of sweat rolled down his brow, but as he backed away his breathing seemed to calm. He looked up, finally noticing the woman standing in the doorway of Ron's bedroom. She hadn't said a word nor did she look frightened, so he slowly backed out of the house, leaving Ron nearly unconscious.

Once John got into his truck and sped off, she felt the coast was clear. The woman squatted down, leaning her head near Ron's. "Now I know that wasn't as good for you as it was for me," she teased with her eyebrows raised, shooting him a look of assurance.

Over at the Slater family home, Megan and Steven had made it back from their date. She'd invited Steven in for some cocktails, being that she wasn't quite ready for their evening to end. Megan entered the living room, carrying two long stem wine glasses in each hand. "Is Merlot okay?" she asked, handing one over to Steven as she sat down next to him on the sofa.

"Merlot is fine... Thank you. Now, you were saying," he said, prompting her to continue their previous conversation.

"Oh... right," she paused to think, "I don't know. I think my marriage fell apart a long time ago. When our daughter was murde..." Megan paused. The words seemed to die in her throat as she glanced up toward the ceiling fan. Images of her daughter hanging there seemed to flash before her eyes. Her hands had begun to tremble. She looked down at her glass, realizing it was nearly sliding from her grip. Megan was about to fall apart right before Steven's eyes. She took a deep breath, forcing herself to collect her emotions. Only she'd completely forgotten what it was she was trying to explain, before her brief meltdown had occurred.

"I'm sorry. Umm... where was I?" she asked with dimming smile, hoping to hide the fact that she was a tad embarrassed.

"Your marriage," Steven replied, then casually sipped his wine, pretending he hadn't noticed the entire debacle.

"Right. We just couldn't pull it together after that. So... here I am."

"I always thought death brought people closer together."

"Not in our case. John... John is my ex-husband's name. He resents me for continuing to live in this house. The house where our daughter was murdered. But, what he doesn't understand is that I can't leave. This is how I keep Samantha with me. Her spirit is here. It has to be. I couldn't just leave her here all alone, with strangers.

Megan gazed into his eyes, searching for signs of empathy. "You understand, right?"

Steven sat his wine glass on the table. "I understand."

"I just really wish things would've gone differently for our family," she continued.

"I don't know. I think everybody has something about their life they'd like to change, but it's the events that occur in our lives that shape us into the people we are today."

At that point, Megan realized that maybe she'd focused more of their conversation than she should have on her soon to be ex-husband. After all, she was on a date with another man. A potential love interest, or so she presumed.

"So if you could go back and change anything, yet still be the same person you are today, what would it be?" she asked, in an attempt at graciously passing him the reins in their conversation.

As Steven pondered her question, his look of compassion flitted into a cold dead stare. His eyes were void of any emotional connection. Although Megan said nothing to address the change in the atmosphere, Steven saw plainly her awareness of his disconnect.

An ominous smirk emerged upon his face as her shoulders began to rise, sinking her chest in toward her back. At last, for the first time during their date, he'd begun to enjoy himself. He closed his eyes, then took a deep breath, savoring the smell of sweat that had begun to overpower her perfume. A corner of her mouth had again started that nervous twitch as Megan came to the realization that she'd made a grave mistake inviting him into her home. Stricken by a wave of panic, Megan stood from the sofa, but it was too late. His eyes had already opened, and the solemn look upon Steven's face did not bode well.

"What would I change? I would have killed you, before I

killed your daughter. You're far more pathetic."

"Oh God!" Megan screamed as she turned to run away. Steven lunged at her, wrapping his hands around her throat.

"Oh God," he mocked her. "I'm pretty sure if he was gonna help, he would have started with your dear old daughter." He proceeded to unleash upon Megan a wrath that Samantha had already suffered.

By then night had fallen, but the pale moon was full and bright as Shawn strolled up his block, immersed in the music blaring from his iPod. Mumbling along to Maroon Five's, Harder to Breathe, he was completely unaware that soon, he himself was about to walk into a trap.

THE FINAL CHAPTER

A few hours later, John had just gotten dressed. After the brutal annihilation he'd bestowed Ron, John took a long shower to wash off the blood, and collect his thoughts. Since he hadn't found what he was looking for in Samantha's belongings, he'd decided he would go to Mr. Schwartz's house to continue his investigation.

When John got into his truck, the first thing he noticed was a tape recorder laying on the passenger seat. It wasn't his. He immediately hopped out of the truck, scanning the area around his vehicle to see if anyone was lurking around. Maybe whomever had left the recorder in the truck was still there watching, he thought. John looked under his vehicle. Nothing was there. He'd found himself in a truly precarious situation. But with no other choice than to face the dilemma head on, John climbed back into the driver's seat.

There was a small note attached to the recorder that read: PLAY ME. John obliged, pressing the play button on the recorder.

"Good evening, John. I see you've been a busy boy. I've been watching you for quite some time now, and after thorough consideration, I've finally decided that I've allowed you to follow me long enough. I really think it's time you get to know me a little better. But, first things first. I'd like you to do something for me. Are you listening? Of course you are." Steven belted out a most sinister laugh. "Listening and watching... watching and listening... John I'd like you to go and check on your family. You remember them, don't you? Your slutty wife and misguided son."

Upon hearing those words, his heart sank into his stomach. John immediately started his truck and sped out of the parking lot, clipping the curb on his way out. The tires burned rubber as he hung a hard left at the corner by his apartment. "Fuck! Fuck! Fuck!" John whaled on his steering wheel in frustration. It took him all of thirteen minutes to make it to the big house on Cozen Drive, speeding and weaving through what little traffic he encountered on his way there. When John pulled up, he slammed on his brakes, screeching tires marked the cement on street in front of the house. John grabbed a flashlight from the glove compartment, then bolted from his truck toward the front door.

The house was dark. All of the lights were out on the inside, as well as the exterior. John slowed his pace as he'd gotten closer, noticing that the door was ajar. For a brief moment he closed his eyes, "Oh God... no," he whispered as feelings of deja vu instantly washed over him. He slowly nudged the door open. His heart felt as if it was going to pound right out of his chest. The thought of him finding his family there slain was almost too much to handle. Beads of sweat had already formed along his brow.

"Shawn! Megan!" he called out to them, before stepping inside. No one answered. John wasn't hesitant to go into the home for fear of being attacked. It was the fear of what he'd lay his eyes upon once he entered. John made it a point never to go back inside that house after he and Megan split.

Nevertheless, it was a feat he'd have to bear.

Once John stepped inside, he flipped the light switch, just as he'd done the night of his daughter's murder, already suspecting it wouldn't illuminate. His suspicions where spot on. John let out a heavy sigh of devastation, before clicking on his flashlight. He flashed the light around the foyer, then up the stairway, just beyond the front door. Still, he saw nothing out of place.

"Megan! Shawn!" he shouted a bit louder. But again, there was nothing.

John made his way over to the entrance of the living room, shining the flashlight along the floor. He took his time, bracing himself, before he'd begun to raise the flashlight. It wasn't long before John had come upon a blood soaked puddle, staining the beige carpet.

"Oh God!"

Dreadfully anticipating the heart wrenching sight he was about to see, he continued to raise the flashlight. "My God," John shook his head in despair, once he'd illuminated Megan's bloody feet, looming in the air. Her toenails were painted a pastel pink. Flashes of Samantha's corpse hanging there, in that very same manner, seemed to come rapid fire through his memory. It felt so real. Still, maybe he was hallucinating, he'd hoped. He jerked the flashlight upward, illuminating her face.

Megan dangled, lifeless, from a braided noose tied from her neck to the ceiling fan. The fan creaked, wobbling as it spun her naked corpse round in circles. Her eyelids were sewn open, her mouth sewn shut. Barbed wire bound her wrists behind her back. Beyond the black and blue bruising, her torso was severely mutilated, covered with small puncture wounds. It was as if her body had been used as a pinata. A section of skin was sliced from her chest plate in the shape of what looked to be a cross. An overwhelming amount of blood had dripped from her body, creating that blood soaked puddle, which stained the beige carpet. Her body was left cold and pale.

Blood spatters canvased everything in the room, the vintage tufted furniture, family portraits, the olive goblet pleated drapes, even the crystal figurines along the fireplace.

John's hands started to tremble. His knee's buckled forcing him to catch his balance along the wall. He touched his hand to his forehead as he'd begun to feel dizzy. When he flashed the light up at Megan a second time, his eyes began to play tricks on him, once more manifesting the memory already etched into his mind. He imagined Samantha hanging there by the braided noose, tied to the wobbling ceiling fan. He closed his eyes tight, shaking the horrifying image from his thoughts.

"Pull it together, John," he quietly coaxed himself. John took a deep breath, then quickly opened his eyes when the one thing that truly mattered settled in his brain. "Shawn... Where's Shawn?"

Again, he moved the light along Megan's hanging corpse, noticing something different. There was a stainless steel letter opener protruding from Megan's belly button, which had been used to attach a note. A note meant specifically for John's eyes.

The lettering on the note had been composed of cut outs from newspaper clippings. He moved closer to Megan, but only enough to see the message clearly, which read: OLD HABITS DIE HARD. COME AND GET YOUR BOY. I'M SURE YOU KNOW WHERE TO FIND ME.

"Son of a bitch!" John shouted angrily. Making a hasty exit, he hoped that it wasn't too late. That his son was still alive. He jumped in his truck, taking off toward his destination.

Since John had recognized the voice on the recorder, he knew exactly where he was expected to go. He'd only ever followed Steven to one place, which was the old abandoned apartment building at the edge of Crimson County. He took every short cut imaginable to make it there as soon as possible, but even in doing so, that ten minute drive seemed as though it took an eternity.

Halfway there, the rain came. John put his wipers on high speed. Still the water washed over the windshield as if it were being poured from buckets, which made his ride even more unnerving. Lightening flashed just a few seconds before the boisterous thunder roared, erupting into a cacophonous crack. A hell of a storm was brewing, much like the fury John harbored.

The entire drive there he thought about all of the time he'd missed with Shawn. He blamed himself for the entire situation. I knew something was fishy about him that night I saw him at the local tavern. I should have killed him then, he thought. John struggled back and forth with the idea, before coming to the conclusion that, at the time, letting Steven live was the only rational decision he could have made. He couldn't just kill someone, having no other reason than suspicion. But, look where that had gotten him. He was left with a dead ex-wife and a son who'd been taken by a maniac. A maniac who'd apparently harbored some sort of sick obsession with he and his family. He'd begun to imagine what a dreadfully meaningless life he would have if Shawn were taken from him, but quickly banished the thought, for it was so unbearable, it had brought him to tears. John sniffled when the mucus ran from his nose, taking it back in, before wiping his face once over with his hand. It'll be fine, he told himself. "Hang on Shawn... I'm coming," he professed, mashing the gas pedal to the floor.

When John arrived at the gates entrance, he noticed that there were only three windows that were lit up, all of which were on the sixth floor. The rest of the building was cloaked in darkness. John drove around back where he figured he wouldn't be seen, due to the storm and lack of light. He got out of his truck, then stuffed his .38 caliber pistol into the back of his pants, under his blue jean jacket. Although the rain had drenched John in just seconds of exiting his vehicle, it hadn't phased him in the least. He was focused on a specific objective, which was finding Shawn and bringing him home safe.

He traveled back to the front of the building on foot. John wasn't sure where or even if, he and Shawn would have to make an escape, so along the way, he checked to make sure none of the exits were blocked from the outside. When

John got to the front of the building, he took out his gun, holding it tight with his right hand, then pulled cautiously on the door handle with his left to open it. "Shit," John blurted in a hushed tone, realizing it was so dark he could barely see inside. He used his foot to prop open the door, so that he was able to use his left hand to grab the small flash light from his jacket pocket.

He clicked on his light, then went inside, gently lifting his foot, allowing the door to close quietly behind him. John was calm. His breathing was steady. He'd been waiting for over a year. Finally, the opportunity to exact his revenge upon the man that killed his daughter had been presented to him. John moved the light along the wall in front of him until he came upon an elevator. He walked over, pressing the button on the wall, but only to see if it was operable. He had no intentions of actually taking the elevator. It worked. When the door opened John quickly flashed the light inside, while at the same time, holding up the gun, ready to shoot if necessary. But, there was no one there. Just as the door was about to close again, John reached in, forcing it back open. He stepped inside, using his foot to keep the door from closing, then illuminated the elevator panel to press the button for the eleventh floor. It would take the elevator all the way to the top, creating the illusion that it was where John was headed. At least that was the plan.

After John stepped out, releasing the elevator, he continued to survey the entryway of the building, bringing him to a stairwell. John looked up, shining the light above him. He lit up the winding stairwell, checking to make sure his way seemed clear enough to travel undetected. He started up the stairwell, headed for the sixth floor, being sure to step as quietly as he possibly could. Once he'd made it there, he moved quickly, taking a peek through the small window on the entry door. Still, he saw nothing, but he didn't want to flash the light for too long, and risk alerting Steven as to his location. John put the flashlight back into his pocket, then turned the knob. Yet, he only pulled the door open enough to slip his body through. The building was old, so naturally John assumed that the rusted hinges on the iron door would screech loudly if widened too far.

He could see just enough to make his way down the hall. It was the light that glowed from underneath the doors of three apartments that guided his way. John came upon the first illuminated apartment, and turned the knob. When he tried to open the door, it wasn't as easy as it should have been, considering it wasn't locked. He had to use a little force, leaning his body against the door to get it to nudge open, even in the slightest. What John didn't realize was that there was a string attached to the top of the door. The other end of that string was attached to another door. One that was affixed to a metal cage. A cage which housed a large rottweiler. The further John pushed the door open, the more the cage door lifted. John didn't open the door completely, but unfortunately it was just enough for the rottweiler to crawl out on its belly.

By the time he'd nudged his way into the apartment, the canine had already leaped onto its hind legs. John turned, alerted by the sound of its growl, but he hadn't the time to brace himself for the ambush that was about to ensue. The brute force of the rottweiler's pounce sent John staggering back, before ultimately being taken to the ground. His gun flew from his grasp, sliding across the floor as he held tight to the dogs collar with both hands, struggling to keep it from sinking its teeth into his flesh. He and the one hundred and thirty pound male rottweiler were nose to snout. John's face burned red as he struggled to push the animal back off of him. It barked and snared mercilessly, leaking saliva onto his face.

"Ahhhhh fuck!!"

John whaled as he turned his cheek, mustering up enough strength to roll the dog from over top of him. He climbed on top of the animal, mashing his fist down on the dog's throat as he held its collar. The rottweiler snarled, and gasped for air. John punched the rottweiler hard in the groin once, twice, and then a third time, before it finally yelped in pain. He stood to his feet, still managing to maintain a firm grasp on the wiggling dog's collar. "Urrrgh," he growled, dragging it across the wood floor. John built up speed as he approached a window, eventually flinging the rottweiler up into the air, and launching it through the glass. He turned his head to shield his face from the shattered pieces. His heart pounded as he bent over, resting his hands upon his knees, composing his winded breaths. It took him a few seconds to gather himself, before he walked over to the busted window to peer down at what he expected to be a regrettable sight.

Fortunately, the animal had fallen to a second rooftop only three levels down. It laid wounded, but still alive. He stepped back, then looked up at the ceiling, letting out a long exhale, "Shit." John shook his head in relief, because thankfully, that particular struggle was over.

He headed across the room to retrieve his gun, but along the way the floor creaked, then SNAP, his right foot broke through a piece of rotted floor board. "Damn it," John whispered angrily, tugging at his leg to free his foot from the hole. After several hard tugs, he managed to pull himself free, but with his right foot still suspended in the air, the section of floor beneath him suddenly collapsed. John's entire body, from his chest down, had been swallowed up by the rotted floor. He dangled into the apartment beneath him. The only thing that held him from falling through completely were his arms, which rested upon the remaining floor.

Although John was afraid he'd fall through if he put more pressure on the wood, he had no choice. He wasn't going to hang there and wait for Steven to come and murder him. But, he was going to need all of the upper body strength he had to get out of that mess. John prayed it didn't send him crashing onto the foundation beneath him. First, he used his elbows, pressing them down onto the wood. That lifted him up enough to support himself with his forearms, which he then used to pull himself up to his waist. John relied on the palms of his hands and the stability in his wrists to raise him up to his thighs, at which point, he was able to raise one knee, then crawl out the rest of the way.

The task had taken a lot out of him. John rolled onto his back, resting on the floor, then let out another sigh of relief. One he'd released a bit too soon, because right then the remaining floor gave way, allowing John and his gun to fall through. "Ahhh!" he yelled, completely caught off guard.

Unfortunately, the condition of the wood on the floor in the apartment beneath him was not any better. John weighed at least one hundred and ninety five pounds, and with him free falling so rapidly, he crashed right through that rotted floor as well. John slammed onto the floor of the large studio apartment on the fourth floor. He shielded his face with his arms as the fragments of rotted wood fell down atop of him. He coughed and gagged, overtaken by the dust and debris in the atmosphere.

John moaned in pain, rolling onto his left side, before pressing his right hand upon his lower back. But he was determined not to lay there wallowing in the pain he felt. So he sat up, shaking his head to free it of debris, then dusted himself off. He grabbed the flashlight out of his jacket pocket, but just as he was about to turn it on, a lamp illuminated.

Steven stood not too far from where he'd fallen. "Nice of you to join us, John." Steven laughed, then proceeded with a slow applause, reveling in the thought that John was a bumbling idiot, and clearly no match for him. "Yes! Now that was a hell of an entrance, my friend!"

Steven glanced off sides, over at Shawn "Give it up for your dear old dad," then directed his attention back to John, "Oh, I forgot, he's a little tied up right now. Don't take it personal. Like I said, it was truly a hell of an entrance. Although, we do have an elevator, you know." Steven winked, then flashed a quick smile.

John focused his eyes on Shawn, pondering his next move. Permeated with the determination to rescue his son, he struggled to his feet. "Are you okay, son?"

When Shawn had entered his home, he'd suffered a blow to the head, knocking him out cold. Blood leaked from his hair, down the back of his neck, out of the wound on his scalp. Although Shawn was standing, he'd been restrained. His ankles were bound together with rope. A separate rope bound his wrists together behind his back, then extended up across a reinforce beam in the ceiling. It yielded an axe, which was propelled in the air. If Shawn were able to somehow untie the rope, the axe was positioned to release, swinging down, ultimately penetrating his chest. Shawn shot his father a beseeching glance, "Get me outta here, Dad," he uttered in a subdued voice, before his eyes began to squint, at which point his chin dropped to his chest. He'd begun to give in to the wooziness he felt.

John stepped forward, intent on releasing him.

"Tsk tsk tsk tsk tsk," Steven clicked his tongue to his teeth, warning John against the decision. "I wouldn't do that if I were you."

Instead, John bolted toward Steven, tackling him to the floor. He climbed on top of him, straddling his belly, then proceeded to pound his fists down on Steven's face. Fueled with rage, the blows came rapidly one after another, after another. Steven's arms laid limp above his head. The blood spewed from his mouth, while more ran down from his nose. John got up, but he wasn't finished. He grabbed Steven by his left wrist and inner thigh. "Ahhh!" John hollered out, rostering the strength to lift him from the floor, only to release him out into the air.

Steven had been launched across the room, into an old dirty sofa. When he'd landed, the sofa tipped backward, allowing his body to roll onto the floor.

John headed for Steven to finish him off, "You son of a bitch, I'm gonna send you straight to hell," he professed.

Behind the cover of the sofa, he laid there with his back to John. Only, Steven was playing possum. He'd already pulled a dart gun from his pants. No sooner than John had stepped behind the sofa, Steven rolled over, pulling the trigger. The dart hit John on his left side. He looked down at the dart wide eyed, in shock. John reacted quickly, pulling the dart out and tossing it across the room. But the serum had already begun to course through his veins. He felt the effects of the neuromuscular blocking agent, instantaneously. "What did you do to me?"

First, his entire body felt warm. He could taste something weird on the back of his tongue. Then his toes started to tingle, at which point he dropped to the floor. John had begun to twitch. Soon he'd lost control of his bladder, which caused urine to run down his leg, dampening the front of his jeans. He tried to talk, yet his voice was so weak you couldn't distinguish a word he was saying.

Steven got up, then cracked his neck from side to side, before spitting a glob of blood from his mouth onto the floor near John. He winced, wiping his nose, "Ouch."

"You got me good there, Johnny boy."

Steven turned the couch upright, then pushed it across the floor, positioning it so that he could sit facing John. He plopped down on the sofa feeling most confident. "This is the best part. We've come to the highlight of our relationship. The part where the protagonist and the antagonist match wits... raw power... skill. Although... I'll admit, you've got me on the raw power part. There's a good reason for that. Since I've been watching you, I can positively say you haven't gotten a single piece of pussy in... What's it been, well over a year now? You've probably got a lot of build up going on down there. I'd be pretty pissed off, too."

"It's obvious that you're not too bright," he remarked, pointing up at the hole in the ceiling.

"Now as far as skill, I'm gonna have to take that trophy as well. I mean... I've killed you twice already. Your daughter, then your ex-wife... I really don't think you can take much more. You know what your problem is? I'll tell you. You thought you were gonna win because you're fighting for good. Your cause is one of righteousness. But at the same time, you could never beat me, John. You know why, John? I'll tell you why." Steven got up from the sofa, "It's because you're weak. You have too... many... weaknesses," he insinuated, pointing the dart gun at Shawn.

"You know," he said, lowering the gun as he turned back to John, "I actually contemplated fucking your ex-wife, before I strangled the life out of her. But, I'd grown tired of listening to her bitching and moaning about your failed marriage. I figured the corpse would be a far more enjoyable lay. For what it's worth though, I think in time you two could have worked things out. You know... sorted out your differences, and what not." Steven paused for a moment, then continued, "Oh well," he brushed off the idea with a shrug of the shoulders and an unrepentant grin.

Steven walked back over toward John. "Look at you now, Johnny boy. I know what you're thinking. What a dilemma you've gotten yourself into," he teased as he knelt by his side. "You were never any match for me. I kill because I crave looking into a person's eyes as they come to the realization that I hold their life in my hands. Just as you look now. Helpless. Pitiful. This, my dear nemesis, has always been my true calling."

Steven's mind drifted, reflecting on memories from his past. Memories that had led him to who he'd come to be.

He was nearly six years old when his angry father tore through his childhood home, searching for him. "Where are you, sissy boy?!" he yelled out, clutching a baby doll in his right hand.

He was wearing jeans, but no shirt. His father was a tall, gangly, bald man, but the pale skin of his torso, all the way up throughout his neck, was covered in tattoos. Snakes, skulls, naked women, even a swastika all had their place among his body art. There was also a large crucifix that had been branded on the skin directly between his chest plates.

"You better get out here now, boy. Don't make me have to come and find you," he warned, before lifting the blanket to look underneath young Steven's bed.

"There you are, sissy boy!" his father shouted as he grabbed young Steven's arm, then dragged him from under the cover of the bed. "Ahhh!" young Steven screamed, while being snatched up through the air, then tossed into the corner like a lap doll. His eyes were beaming with fear. He trembled like a wet puppy.

"What did I tell you about playing with these things?" he asked, launching the doll at him.

"I didn't, Daddy. I promise," young Steven pleaded. His father unlatched his leather belt, sliding it from around his waist, "Don't you lie to me, boy," he threatened, wagging the belt from left to right.

Young Steven lifted his knees, tucking his head into his lap to brace himself for the beating, he knew was inevitable. His father held the belt over his head, wheel-ding it down time after time on his arms and legs. Welts and bruises showed up almost instantly on his frail body.

Later that same day, young Steven was outside throwing rocks in his backyard, when he saw the glare from a pair of eyes hiding beneath some loose foliage, next to his garage. Intrigued, he sat down, Indian style, on the ground nearby. "Here kitty kitty," he sang in a soft voice, coaxing the kitten his way. It worked. The malnourished kitten came out of its hiding place, then slowly made its way over to young Steven.

He picked it up and gently rubbed the feline against his cheek, then took a deep breath, basking in the aroma of its fur. He rubbed across the top of its tiny head with his thumb. The kitten purred as young Steven caressed its chin. "Poor, little kitty... You must be starving."

"1212 Destiny Rd," young Steven read from the charm on its collar. "You must be lost. I bet you have a family out there who loves you," he assumed, wishing he had the same. Young Steven grabbed the kitten's collar tight, making a fist, then turned his hand inward, forcing the collar to tightening more and more, choking the life from the little kitten. Controlling whether or not the animal would live or die granted him a feeling of power, moreover comfort. A comfort he hadn't felt, since before his mother walked out on he and his father. Steven was just five years old at the time of his mother's disappearance.

Another memory took hold. Steven was twelve. His father kicked open his bedroom door as he laid in bed, starring at the ceiling. "Let's go, boy," he said waving his whiskey bottle, ushering him to come along. Steven got out of bed, then followed his father down the hall to another bedroom in their small rickety house. Father opened the door to a woman laying on his bed, passed out drunk, and nearly naked. "Have fun," his father instructed, before pushing Steven into the room, and slamming the door behind him. Steven walked over, then sat on the edge of the bed next to her. "Hey, lady," he called out, attempting to see if she were dead or alive. Her frail body laid there limp. Her rib cage protruded against her skin. Steven put his ear to her chest to hear her heartbeat. It was slow and shallow.

"Come on, man... Just let us go," Shawn pleaded, jolting Steven back to reality from his brief trip down memory lane.

"I'm trying to teach your father a valuable lesson here, Shawn. Weakness is a weed that spreads. You have to gut it out from the root, John. Shawn is one of those weeds."

John struggled to move, however, all that could be mustered was a single tear. It dropped from the corner of his eye, hitting the floor, coupling with his drool which had already collected into a small puddle.

"That's the spirit, John!" Steven said, welcoming John's efforts to fight back. "Watch this," he stood, then headed in Shawn's direction.

"I'm sending you to a much better place. Where you can be with your mom and sister. Soon after, your father will follow. Then all of you can be together again. Then you'll have finally broken free from the misery of your life," Steven professed as he stood eye to eye with Shawn.

"Don't patronize me."

Riled by Shawn's back talk, Steven grabbed a hold of Shawn's face, squeezing his jaws.

"You don't have to thank me. That's what I'm here for. You're not cut out for this anyway," he whispered. Steven released his hold on Shawn's face, belting out a sinister chuckle as he furnished his cheek a few light slaps. "Are you ready to die, Shawn?"

Shawn leaned his head in closer to Steven's. Their noses nearly touched. "Are you?" he countered, with a calm, calculated voice. Steven's smile dimmed as a puzzled expression surfaced upon his face. He'd recognized a change in Shawn's demeanor. "Huh," he huffed, raising an eyebrow. This kid's got some balls, he thought.

Steven was completely oblivious to the fact that while he was busy spouting off at the mouth, Shawn had managed to retrieve the blade that John had given him from a holster tucked into his pants. He clutched the rope with one hand, then rubbed the knife back and forth across the rope, a few inches below the area he held tight.

"And how do you plan to..." Before Steven could even complete his query, the axe swung down, chopping him in the back. Steven's eyes grew wide with shock. He was in complete disbelief of what had happened. He stumbled back. Spinning in circles, he reached behind him, desperately trying to remove the axe from between his shoulder blades. Meanwhile, Shawn freed his ankles from the rope which bound them.

Shawn leaped into the air, kicking the head of the axe deeper into his back. Blood trickled from Steven's mouth, just before he fell forward onto the floor. Shawn nudged him with his foot, rolling him over onto his side. He knelt near by, starring him in his fear filled eyes.

"You don't have to thank me. That's what I'm here for," he teased, while witnessing his life slip away.

Shawn got up, rushing over to his father. "It's over, Dad. Everything's gonna be okay now. I'm gonna get you some help," he assured John, patting him on the back.

At long last, the man whom had compelled him to murder was dead.

On the day that Megan's funeral had come, John and Shawn were in John's apartment. However, it looked very different. There was no clutter scattered about the floor. No books or newspapers clippings lining the walls... John had cleaned it all out. He and Shawn were starting over. It was just the two of them.

John stood in front of the bathroom mirror, fixing his tie. He was dressed in a black suit with a white collared button up shirt. "You know... I'm glad you've made yourself at home here, son. In my bedroom," he said, emphasizing the word my. "But seriously, we're gonna need a bigger apartment. I don't think your old man's back can take much more of that sofa," he called out to Shawn elsewhere in the apartment.

John wanted to keep Shawn in the best spirits possible, considering he'd just lost his mother, and her funeral was just hours away. Not to mention the fact that he had taken someone's life. Even though John felt Steven didn't deserve to live, he knew from experience that killing someone could take a disastrous toll on an individual's mental state. So all that day, he tried keeping a conversation going, even when they weren't in the same room. The silence between them seemed haunting. John wondered whether or not his son was doing okay. He worried what state of mind Shawn may have been in. "Shawn, you almost ready?" John inquired, hoping to rush Shawn back into his presence.

Shawn was in his father's bedroom. He'd just placed a

framed picture on the immaculately clean dresser. It was a picture of he and Samantha, by the lake. The two of them couldn't have been more than twelve or thirteen years old. They were leaned in cheek to cheek. Both had huge smiles on their faces. We were so happy then, he thought. It was a lifetime ago.

Shawn straightened his suit coat, then began fixing his tie. All of a sudden, the expression on his face shifted from one of complacence to an ominous glare as he gazed at his reflection in the mirror. Lost in a daydream, a recollection of events played out rapidly throughout his psyche.

He stood in the woods at the wee hours of the morning, putting on a ski mask. Shawn watched as Jennifer walked through the woods. He remembered brutally bashing her head in with the boulder, before he'd snatched off her necklace.

Shawn remembered taking the necklace out of his pocket, right before coming through the entrance at the police station. He recalled purposely bumping into an angry Mr. Schwartz, then dropping the necklace into his jacket pocket.

Shawn recollected climbing into Mrs. Schwartz's living room window that fateful night. He could hear the shower running, from the entryway. He bent over retrieving her purse and keys off of the foyer floor, just as Minkzy came along, brushing against his leg. He picked up the cat, carrying it along with him as he walked up the stairs, and into her bedroom. His head tilted as he starred at her closet door. It was at that moment, he'd come up with an idea of how to execute her demise.

He remembered watching Derrick's car blow up as he stood at the woods edge. He put on his hood, picked up his duffel bag, and backed into the darkness as the chaos played out.

Shawn drifted back into the present, smoothing his tie down flat. It was all a lifetime ago, he thought.

"I'm ready," he finally answered, admiring his reflection. Reveling in confidence, he furnished himself a wink. Then a sinister grin emerged with ease. Shawn strolled out of the bedroom, quite certain that he'd gotten away with murder.

THE END

94548087R00117

Made in the USA
Columbia, SC
29 April 2018